The Great Treehouse War

Lisa Graff

Philomel Books

Also by Lisa Graff

A Clatter of Jars

Lost in the Sun

Absolutely Almost

A Tangle of Knots

Double Dog Dare

Sophie Simon Solves Them All

Umbrella Summer

The Life and Crimes of Bernetta Wallflower

The Thing About Georgie

PHILOMEL BOOKS
an imprint of Penguin Random House LLC
375 Hudson Street, New York, NY 10014

Copyright © 2017 by Lisa Graff. Interior illustrations © 2017 by Siobhán Gallagher.
Penguin supports copyright. Copyright fuels creativity, encourages diverse voices,
promotes free speech, and creates a vibrant culture. Thank you for buying an authorized
edition of this book and for complying with copyright laws by not reproducing,
scanning, or distributing any part of it in any form without permission. You are
supporting writers and allowing Penguin to continue to publish books for every reader.

Philomel Books is a registered trademark of Penguin Random House LLC.

Library of Congress Cataloging-in-Publication Data
Names: Graff, Lisa (Lisa Colleen), 1981– author. | Title: The Great Treehouse War /
Lisa Graff. | Description: New York, NY : Philomel Books, [2017] | Summary: Fifth-
grader Winnie, with notes from her friends, writes of turning her treehouse into an
embassy after her newly-divorced parents become unreasonable, where she is joined by
nine others with complaints. | Identifiers: LCCN 2016030937 | ISBN 9780399175008
(hardback) | Subjects: | CYAC: Interpersonal relations—Fiction. | Parents—Fiction. |
Divorce—Fiction. | Friendship—Fiction. | Tree houses—Fiction. | Humorous stories.
| BISAC: JUVENILE FICTION / Family / Marriage & Divorce. | JUVENILE
FICTION / Social Issues / Friendship. | JUVENILE FICTION / Social Issues /
Emotions & Feelings. | Classification: LCC PZ7.G751577 Win 2017 | DDC [Fic]—dc23 |
LC record available at https://lccn.loc.gov/2016030937

Printed in the United States of America. ISBN 9780399175008
1 3 5 7 9 10 8 6 4 2

Edited by Jill Santopolo. Design by Jennifer Chung.
Text set in 12-point Granjon LT Std.

To Beth

(With special thanks to the students of Villa Madonna Academy, Millington Elementary School, and Greenwich Academy, for letting me use some of their best treehouse ideas—and a few of their names, too!)

Mr. B— Here's our submission for the collective memoir contest. Everyone ~~contribbeted~~ contributed, but I did most of the writing. I tried to write it like a normal book, even though a lot of it is about me (that wasn't meant to be braggy, just the truth). Also, lots of people had notes about stuff (especially Squizzy), so I left those on so you could see them before we submit it.

Even if we don't win the contest, I think we did a pretty good job. It turns out we had a lot to write about!

—Winnie

P.S. We DID pass 5th grade, right??

(Please don't flunk us!!!!!)

"Treehouse 10" End Two-Week Siege

Wednesday, May 3rd
BY MARGARET WEINSNOGGLE

GLENBROOK—Parents around the world breathed sighs of relief this morning, as the second to last of the so-called Treehouse 10—all fifth-graders from local Tulip Street Elementary School—ended their 19-day standoff. Cheers could be heard from blocks away when the ninth child climbed down from the treehouse between the properties of Dr. Alexis Maraj and Dr. Varun Malladi, running to hug his tearful parents.

Everyone seemed relieved that the disagreement had at last come to a peaceful end.

Only one member of the Treehouse Ten still refuses to return to American soil. As of press time, Winifred Malladi-Maraj, the treehouse's original resident, remains inside, with no sign of when she might leave. Neither of Winifred's parents chose to comment.

Part I

How It All Started

Tulip Street Ten
(As Drawn by Winnie)

Pencils in his pocket (does he even use them??)

Test tube for experiment he's working on

Aayush Asad

Very curly hair

Pet bird

Pet turtle

Pet pug dog

Pet fish

Tabitha Borchers

Most acrobatic kid in class (if there's something, he'll climb it!)

Brogan Litz

← TWINS! →

Always telling jokes

HA HA HA!

Water balloons

Logan Litz

Winnie— Can you draw me with a lizard too?
—Tabitha

Winnie, I don't think you should draw a lizard because Tabitha doesn't own one. This is supposed to be a <u>memoir</u>. Memoirs are <u>fact</u>. —Squizzy

But lizards are cool! I bet more people will read this book if there are lizards in it!
—Tabitha

TULIP STREET ELEMENTARY SCHOOL

Where every child gets to bloom

360 South Tulip Street, Glenbrook, Pennsylvania 19066

A Note from Mr. Benetto
Fifth Grade Teacher, Room 5L

September 29th

Dr. Alexis Maraj
1 Circle Road
Glenbrook, PA 19066

Dr. Varun Malladi
2 Circle Road
Glenbrook, PA 19066

Dear Dr. Maraj and Dr. Malladi,

I'm writing in regards to your daughter, Winifred Malladi-Maraj. As I mentioned to each of you in our separate parent-teacher conferences after the first week of school, Winnie is smart, curious, and charming, and gets along well with the other students. Most days, however, Winnie is somewhat quiet. At first I believed this to simply be her nature. In my many years as a teacher, I have known many quiet students. And then I noticed something peculiar.

The minute Winnie walked through the door to Room 5L on the first Thursday of school, her face was brighter. All day she was more talkative, more eager to engage. It was as though someone had flipped a switch and brought this previously shy girl to radiant life. I thought that perhaps something amazing had happened the evening before to make her so cheerful. The next day, Winnie was back to her quiet self, and I thought no more of the situation . . . until the following Thursday, when Winnie was once again as carefree as ever. Something, clearly, had happened the evening before—something absolutely wonderful. The following day, the switch flipped back, and once again she withdrew.

I must admit that this morning, on our third Thursday together, I sat at my desk waiting to see which Winnie would walk through the door. And I am both delighted and puzzled to report that it was the happy Winnie—the girl full of sunshine. It's not bad, this weekly change in Winnie, but it is rather curious, and I was hoping the two of you might be able to shed some light on the situation. If there is indeed something on that occurs each Wednesday to make Winnie so delighted, perhaps it might be possible to bring whatever this thing is into her life every day.

I suppose my question to the both of you, then (and I don't mean to pry—understand I simply ask in the best interest of your daughter), is this:

What happens to Winnie on Wednesdays?

Yours sincerely,
Hector Benetto

The Last Day of Fourth Grade

a year before what happened happened

There are a lot of things you should probably know to understand why a bunch of kids decided to climb up a treehouse and not come down. But to really understand it, you'd have to go way back in time, and peek through the living room window of a girl named Winifred Malladi-Maraj, on her last day of fourth grade. Since time travel isn't possible, you'll just have to picture things. So picture this:

After walking home from school, Winnie stepped through the front door, with her backpack over her shoulder. Winnie's parents were sitting on the living room couch, with their hands in their laps. They were watching the front door, like they'd been waiting for their daughter for a long time.

Winnie pulled off her backpack and dropped it in the doorway. Buttons, who is the world's greatest cat, wove his way between Winnie's legs, like he knew she was about to need

Actually, Winnie, some scientists think that time travel IS possible. If you

Aayush, this is a memoir, not a science book! No one cares about time travel! —Squizzy snuggling. "Mom?" Winnie said, squinting her eyes at her parents on the couch. "Dad?" She could tell right away that something weird was going on.

It's probably important to know that Winnie's parents have never been exactly *normal*. Like, instead of playing board games after dinner, the way some families did, Winnie's dad—a biologist—might sit her down for a slide show about his latest research on the beneficial properties of bat guano, which only made Winnie wish she'd never eaten dinner at all. Or Winnie's mom—a mathematician—might try to explain her current work on the Conway's thrackle conjecture, which only made Winnie wish she'd never grown ears.

(Once, Winnie made the mistake of asking if she and her parents could play Boggle after dinner, and afterward she'd had to sit through a two-hour presentation of all of her parents' many awards and grants—none of which, they informed Winnie, had been won playing *Boggle*—and a four-hour argument about whether or not Winnie's dad had more awards than Winnie's mom because there were simply more prizes for biologists than there were for mathematicians.)

(Winnie never asked about Boggle again.)

But finding her parents waiting for her on the couch together seemed *especially* weird to Winnie. Because, normally, Winnie's parents weren't even home when she got out of school. Normally, Winnie started her homework all by herself and then

Winnie, maybe write here that "guano" is another word for "poop"?
—Squizzy

Um, GROSS. We can't write "poop" in our memoir!
—Greta

heated water on the stove exactly at 5:55 p.m., so the pot would be boiling and ready to put pasta in as soon as they got home. (Winnie's parents were very precise about mealtimes.)

(They were very precise about a lot of stuff.)

Another weird thing Winnie noticed that afternoon was the way her parents were sitting. While she was standing in the doorway with Buttons weaving between her legs, she realized that she hadn't ever seen both of her parents on the same couch before. When they watched television or sat with guests, Winnie's mom usually squished herself against one couch arm, while her dad sat in the recliner on the far side of the room.

"What's going on?" Winnie asked. Even Buttons let out a confused *mew?*

"Come sit down," Winnie's mom replied, patting the couch cushion between herself and Winnie's dad.

"Yes," Winnie's dad agreed. (That was another weird thing, Winnie noticed. Her parents *never* agreed.) "Have a seat. We marked a spot for you."

And *that* was the weirdest thing of all. There was a tiny X of masking tape stuck to the center of the middle couch cushion. Her parents, Winnie realized as she stepped closer, had measured out a spot for her, so that she'd be sitting exactly evenly between them—not one millimeter closer to one than the other.

But Winnie, who was pretty used to her parents being weird, decided there was nothing to do but sit. Buttons sat, too, hopping right into her lap.

"Winifred," her mom said. She cleared her throat. "Your father and I—"

"Oh no," Winnie's dad cut in, putting up a hand to stop Winnie's mom. "We agreed *I* would tell her. You got to tell Winifred about the tooth fairy."

Winnie's mom frowned. "I don't see how that's pertinent, Varun. This is an entirely different—"

"We *discussed* this," Winnie's dad argued. "But once again, you're attempting to ruin—"

While Winnie's parents argued, Buttons purred a little louder in Winnie's lap, scrunching his head under her hand. Winnie scratched and scratched at Buttons's soft orange fur, while her parents argued and argued. Winnie watched her mom, so angry with her dad. She watched her dad, so furious with her mom. Her parents might have been acting weird, Winnie realized, but the fighting, *that* was completely normal.

And when she realized that, Winnie knew, deep in her gut, precisely why her parents had sat her down on that tiny X of masking tape.

"You guys are getting a divorce, aren't you?" she asked them.

Her parents stopped fighting at once. They turned, both together, and they stared at her.

"That's the thing you were going to tell me, right?" Winnie said.

"Yes," Winnie's mom said, putting a hand on Winnie's knee. "But don't worry. We have a very sensible plan for how to divide your time equally between the two of us."

Winnie's dad put a hand on Winnie's other knee. "*Exactly* evenly," he told her.

For the next half an hour, Winnie sat precisely between her two parents, with one of their hands on each of her knees, as they explained their very sensible plan for her future.

They'd found an unusual street, they told Winnie, a "real gold mine," called Circle Road, just one block over from Winnie's uncle Huck's house.

Winnie scratched a little harder at Buttons's neck.

Circle Road, Winnie's parents explained, looped around on itself in a tiny circle, so that there was just enough space for two houses.

Winnie stroked Buttons's soft belly.

Winnie's mom would live in the two-story Colonial on the northernmost end of the circle, and Winnie would stay with her on Sundays, Tuesdays, and Fridays.

Winnie caressed the base of Buttons's ears, just the way he liked.

Her dad would live on the southernmost side of the street, in the yellow split-level (which might have *seemed* smaller than Winnie's mom's house, he informed his daughter, but was technically bigger, because of the square footage of the basement). Winnie would stay with him on Mondays, Thursdays, and Saturdays.

Winnie rubbed under Buttons's orange chin.

Both houses had sprawling backyards, they went on, which backed up onto each other.

Winnie nestled her cheek in the soft fur at the base of Buttons's neck.

And at the exact center of Circle Road, her parents said, smack in between the two houses—and definitely *not* (they'd checked) on either parent's property—was an enormous linden tree, with thick branches that reached in all directions. That's where Winnie would stay on Wednesdays.

Winnie must've squeezed Buttons a little too tightly then, because he let out an angry *mew!*

"I'm going to live in a *tree?*" Winnie asked her parents. It was the first thing she'd said in thirty minutes.

"Don't be ridiculous," her mom said.

"You'll be in a *treehouse*," her dad clarified. "Your uncle Huck has already agreed to design it."

Hearing that made Winnie and Buttons feel a little bit better, because Uncle Huck was both an amazing uncle and a fabulous architect. (He was also the one who'd taught Winnie all about Artist Vision, which was something that would definitely come in handy later.) But still . . .

"You really want me to live in a treehouse *every Wednesday*?" Winnie asked, glancing from her mom to her dad and back again. "All by myself?"

"It's the only way to split things evenly," her dad replied. "Since every week has seven days in it. Seven, you know, is not an even number."

"Yes," Winnie's mom said. "We went over and over it. That's the only way it works. Three days with your father, three days with me, and one day on your own. Doesn't that sound like a very sensible plan?"

"Um . . . ," Winnie began, glancing from her dad to her mom and back again. Buttons wasn't quite sure how he felt about things, either. "I guess?" she said at last.

"I knew you'd think so," her dad said with a smile. "It was my idea, after all."

"*Your* idea?" Winnie's mom cried. "I very much disagree with *that* statement, Varun."

"Oh, *do* you?" Winnie's dad said. "What a shock, Alexis, that you feel the need to disagree with me."

"I'll disagree with you when you take claim to *my* proposals, Varun."

As her parents continued their argument, Winnie scooped

up Buttons and headed down the hallway to her room. Neither of her parents seemed to notice that she'd left. Winnie shut the door on their bickering, thinking that perhaps it wouldn't be so bad after all, having one day a week to herself.

•

A Map of the Neighborhood
(As Drawn by Winnie)

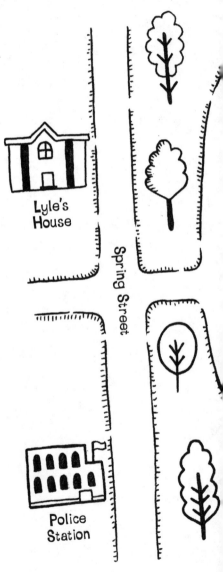

Lyle's
House

Spring Street

Police
Station

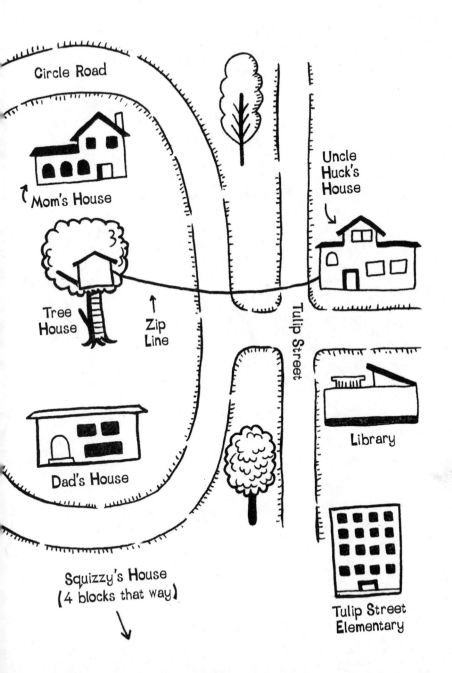

Circle Road

Mom's House

Uncle Huck's House

Tree House

Zip Line

Tulip Street

Dad's House

Library

Squizzy's House
(4 blocks that way)

Tulip Street Elementary

Winnie's Treehouse
(As Designed by Huck Maraj and Drawn by Winnie)

First Floor

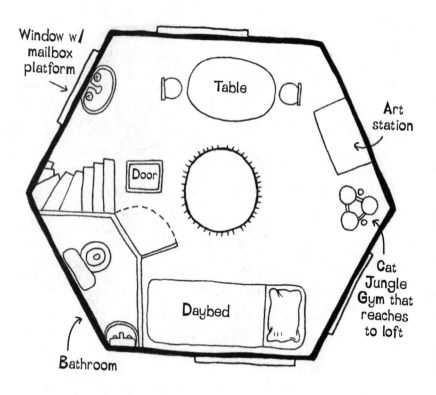

Window w/ mailbox platform

Table

Art station

Door

Cat Jungle Gym that reaches to loft

Daybed

Bathroom

Loft

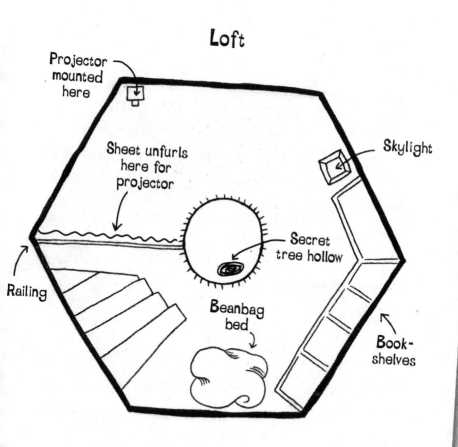

Projector mounted here

Sheet unfurls here for projector

Skylight

Secret tree hollow

Railing

Beanbag bed

Book-shelves

A Nothing-Special
Wednesday
2 days before what happened happened

The Wednesday before what happened happened—April 12th, to be exact—Winnie had no idea that it was any special day at all. Maybe, if she'd known, she would've done things differently. Maybe, after school, she would've raced to her treehouse even quicker than normal, in eight minutes instead of nine. But since there was no way for her to know what was going to happen, she acted like it was just any other, nothing-special Wednesday.

When she reached the linden tree between her parents' two yards, Winnie grabbed hold of the rope ladder that clung to the trunk and stuck one foot on the bottom rung. Then she hoisted herself up, quick as a monkey. The treehouse stood about fifteen feet off the ground, so it was a long rope-trek, but Winnie had been climbing it every Wednesday for nearly a year, so she was good at it. Just before she reached the bottom of the treehouse,

Well, Winnie could have known, technically, if she came back from the future to tell herself. Time machines aren't real yet, but scientists think

NO ONE CARES, AAYUSH!!! —Squizzy

✓ Geckos climb even faster than monkeys, because of their hairy feet. (Lizards rule!) —Tabitha

✓ if all it takes is hairy feet, then my brother kyle should try mount everest. —logan

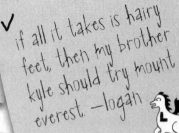

✓ Good one, Lo. —Brogan

where the under-porch scooped out a little hollow for sitting and unlatching the trapdoor, Winnie reached out her left hand to rub the bronze plaque that had been hammered into the tree's trunk long, long ago.

Planted by the
Republic of Fittizio
1863

That's what the plaque said. Winnie had looked it up once, and it turned out that the Republic of Fittizio was a former country in Western Europe, which had gone belly-up over a hundred years before Winnie was even born. Winnie had no idea why someone from a now-extinct country would've planted a tree in her hometown, far away in suburban Philadelphia, but having the plaque there made her tree feel even more special, so she always gave it a little rub when she climbed past, for good luck.

Winnie spun the combination on the trapdoor's padlock and pushed her way inside the treehouse. Buttons was sitting in the middle of the treehouse floor, licking one paw and waiting for her. Just like Winnie, Buttons moved from house to house every day of the week—Sundays, Tuesdays, and Fridays at Winnie's mom's, and Mondays, Thursdays, and Saturdays at

Winnie, can you make sure everyone knows this is the kind of plaque like a sign, not the kind on your teeth? So they don't get worried.
—Lyle

Lyle, you are so <u>weird.</u>
— Squizzy

I knew why! (But Winnie didn't, because she hadn't read my local history report yet.)
— Squizzy

Winnie's dad's. On Wednesdays he climbed the branches of the linden tree and squeezed through a cat door just beyond the human entrance, keeping guard till Winnie joined him.

The first thing Winnie did when she got inside (since she still thought it was a nothing-special Wednesday, same as every week), was cross to the kitchen area and grab a snack. The treehouse was pretty big—maybe six and a half kid-lengths wide. The thick trunk of the linden tree ran through the center of the house, all the way up to the second floor, and out the top of the roof, and it was an excellent spot to tack up doodles and drawings. Those weren't the only decorations in the treehouse, though. When she'd first moved in, Uncle Huck had helped Winnie paint each wall different colors—turquoise blue with white polka dots, pink with wiggly green stripes—whatever she'd felt like. No matter what the weather was outside, the inside of the treehouse was always bright and cheerful.

Winnie opened the mini fridge and pulled out a carton of milk. From the cupboard above the sink, she grabbed a green bowl, a spoon, and a box of Froot Loops, and then she sat down at the small round table. Buttons settled himself on top of the table, like a fluffy kitty king. There was no oven or stove in the treehouse, since Uncle Huck had been worried about Winnie setting the linden on fire (what with Winnie being only eleven and everything). But there *was* a toaster oven and an electric teakettle, which Winnie mainly used for making hot cocoa.

The only problem with Winnie is that her favorite type of hot chocolate is the kind with the mini marshmallows. Everyone knows the dark chocolate one is the best. —Squizzy

Wrong! Sugar-free hot cocoa is better than anything. —Lyle

Winnie shook the last of the Froot Loops from the box and wolfed them down, then pushed the bowl to Buttons, who lapped up the speckly milk. After finishing their snack, Winnie and Buttons checked the "mailbox."

The mailbox was really a large platform that Uncle Huck had rigged to a pulley. If someone left Winnie a letter or a package, they'd push a button that lit the red lightbulb near Winnie's kitchen window. Then all Winnie had to do was open the window and haul the platform up. Uncle Huck often left Winnie a treat or two on Wednesday afternoons—a cooler of lemonade for her fridge, or a couple of ham sandwiches for her and Buttons (Buttons was awfully fond of ham sandwiches). That afternoon, there was a fresh box of Froot Loops and a brand-new sketchbook. Winnie hugged the sketchbook to her chest and took a whiff of its fresh-paper smell. Somehow Uncle Huck always seemed to know exactly what she needed, even before she thought of it herself.

For a moment, Winnie considered climbing out the window and onto the roof, where Uncle Huck had installed a two-way zip line that ran directly between her treehouse and his home, one block away. It would be the fastest way to drop in and say thanks. But in the end she decided against it. Thinking it was a nothing-special Wednesday, Winnie decided to do all the nothing-special things she normally did (which were really kind of special, after all).

I wish I'd decided against using that thing. Ouch! —Brogan

As far as Winnie was concerned, the only problem with Wednesdays was that there was only one of them a week. Which made it super difficult to figure out how to fill that day up. That Wednesday, for example, Winnie had doodling to do and hot cocoa to make and the world's greatest cat to snuggle. She also had a week's worth of homework to catch up on and tests to study for and an entire book to read for a book report. Not to mention that she really ought to figure out an amazing present for Squizzy's birthday the next day and sort through all her swimsuits to find the perfect one for Lyle's pool party in June. On nothing-special Wednesdays, Winnie often ended up doing the sorts of things that *most* kids could do any old day of the week.

At first, dividing her days between her parents had worked perfectly. Spending *exactly equal* time with each parent meant that Winnie only had to be around one of them at once, which was good for everyone, because whenever her parents were in the same room together, they always found some way to drive Winnie crazy. (One time, at the Parents' Night Concert, Winnie's dad was seated two rows farther back from the stage than Winnie's mom, and he made such a stink that Greta's great-grandma finally switched with him.) So at first, the "very sensible plan" Winnie's parents had thought up seemed like a total success.

Yay! —Squizzy

✓

Yeah, Nana's still pretty peeved about that. —Greta

And then Winnie's mom remembered about Thanksgiving.

Before the divorce, no one in Winnie's family had ever cared about most holidays, like Easter or Hanukkah or Diwali. The only one they celebrated at all was Thanksgiving. Before the divorce, they always had a huge family feast. Winnie's mom would make turkey and cranberries and four kinds of potatoes, and Winnie's dad would prepare sausage stuffing completely from scratch. Uncle Huck brought his famous blackberry pie—Winnie's favorite dessert on the planet—and they'd spend the day talking and toasting and telling stories and stuffing themselves silly. Back then, Winnie figured that if you were only going to celebrate one holiday a year, Thanksgiving was a good one to pick.

So maybe it shouldn't have been too surprising that when Winnie's mom realized she was never going to celebrate Thanksgiving with her daughter again (because of Winnie's dad always having Thursdays, because of Winnie's parents' "very sensible plan"), she decided to pick a new holiday to celebrate and to make it even *better* than Thanksgiving. To make Winnie "forget all about that silly dinner with your father."

The holiday Winnie's mom picked was Flag Day.

Winnie's mom didn't *ask* Winnie if she wanted to celebrate

Flag Day. Instead, she packed her daughter in the car that Tuesday afternoon and drove her to the local dedication ceremony of the new flag retirement box outside the sheriff's office. (The ceremony was about as boring as that last sentence.)

"Isn't this just as much fun as Thanksgiving?" her mom asked her when they were back at the house, designing their own flags and sporting silly bonnets like Betsy Ross.

Winnie could tell that it was important to her mom that Flag Day be a super-incredible holiday. And really, Winnie figured, what did it hurt to lie a little, just to make her mom happy? So she told her, "Yeah, Mom. Flag Day is *amazing*. Even better than Thanksgiving."

Well.

Maybe Winnie should've known. Maybe she should've predicted that her mom would call her dad and brag that she'd found a holiday to celebrate with their daughter that was even more stupendous than the one *he* was stuck with. Maybe Winnie should have figured that, once her dad heard the news, he'd devote weeks of his life to researching little-known holidays online so that he could one-up Winnie's mom. Maybe Winnie should have imagined that just a few Saturdays later, she'd be spending an evening in her dad's backyard, camping out in sleeping bags and peering through binoculars for signs of extraterrestrial life, to celebrate World UFO Day.

And, okay, World UFO Day *was* actually pretty fun. Winnie and her dad snacked on space ice cream and made up their own goofy alien language. They played Ultimate UFO Frisbee and stayed up late into the evening, watching the stars.

The problem was that Winnie's mom *saw* them celebrating World UFO Day from the window of her den. (Winnie would later wonder if her dad had secretly planned on that happening all along.) Which, of course, led Winnie's mom to research more unique holidays of her own.

And that's when things really started to get bonkers.

Some of the holidays Winnie and her mom celebrated were awesome, like Ice Cream Sandwich Day.

Some of the holidays were . . . *unusual*, like Cow Appreciation Day.

And some of the holidays were ones Winnie wished she had never, ever heard of, like Underwear Day.

Winnie did her best to keep the new holidays a secret from her dad, but he found out anyway. (Winnie would later wonder if her mom didn't specifically plan a parade for Lasagna Day in order to rub her dad's face in their party.) So before long, Winnie was observing even *more* obscure holidays with her father.

Sand Castle Day.

Bad Poetry Day.

Rad!. —Aayush

✓
Um, ew, that is not
a real holiday.
—Greta

✓
Logan, we are TOTALLY
celebrating Underwear
Day next year!
—Brogan

Burger Day.

The more holidays her dad found, the more her mom did.

The more holidays her mom found, the more her dad did.

When Winnie's mom took her to the boardwalk for a blowout Roller Coaster Day bash, Winnie's father responded with a full-on fiesta for Take Your Cat to the Vet Day. (Buttons wasn't too excited about that one.) By the time Winnie started fifth grade at Tulip Street Elementary, she was celebrating a holiday every day of the week—except, of course, on Wednesdays. And it wasn't that Winnie didn't *like* holidays. But tossing hundreds of Slinkies down the stairwell over and over for National Slinky Day meant that there was very little time left in Winnie's afternoon to do anything else. Her parents were so focused on making sure that every single day they spent with their daughter was better than any day she spent with her *other* parent, that Winnie never had a spare second to doodle in her sketchbook or hang out with her friends or even finish her homework. 🌀

Except of course on Wednesdays.

So *that* Wednesday, the nothing-special Wednesday, Winnie did exactly what she wanted. She snagged some supplies from her art station (where there was an easel and tons of paper and paintbrushes and pipe cleaners and pretty much every art supply you could think of), walked by the "lounging area" with the daybed and the teeny-tiny bathroom, and climbed the steps

I wish my parents forced me to play with Slinkies instead of doing my homework.
—Joey

to the second-floor loft. There she flopped down on her giant beanbag bed and opened up her new sketchbook from Uncle Huck. The book's unlined pages seemed full of possibility, inviting Winnie to draw any doodle she wanted or tell any story that popped into her brain. Buttons scrambled up his cat jungle gym to snuggle in beside her, and together they spent that Wednesday afternoon thinking and doodling and staring out the window and really doing nothing special at all.

When the sky outside grew dark and the air grew still, Winnie and Buttons tucked themselves under the soft, ratty quilt that had once been her baby blanket, and Winnie set the sketchbook full of brand-new, nothing-special doodles on the nearby shelf. They gazed out the skylight above them, watching the leaves and the stars and the world, keeping each other company in comfortable quiet.

Maybe, if Winnie had known what was about to happen, she would have stayed awake a little longer, breathing in the nothing-special treehouse smell, listening to the soft chirp of the nothing-special crickets outside. But she didn't. So instead she drifted off into a perfectly lovely, nothing-special sleep.

APRIL!!

Mom's House
DAD'S HOUSE
Treehouse

SUNDAY	MONDAY	TUESDAY
2 Peanut Butter & Jelly Day!	3 TWEED DAY!	4 Vitamin C Day!
9 Winston Churchill Day!	10 INTER- NATIONAL SAFETY PIN DAY!	11 Barbershop Quartet Day!
16 Eggs Benedict Day!	17 BAT APPRECIATION DAY!	18 Amateur Radio Day!
23 Talk Like Shakespeare Day!	24 PIG IN A BLANKET DAY!	25 Hug a Plumber Day!
30 National Raisin Day!		

WEDNESDAY	THURSDAY	FRIDAY	SATURDAY
			1 SOURDOUGH BREAD DAY!
5 work on local history report?	6 CARAMEL POPCORN DAY!	7 Beaver Day!	8 DRAW A PICTURE OF A BIRD DAY!
12 snuggle with Buttons	13 NATIONAL PEACH COBBLER DAY!	14 Dolphin Day!	15 RUBBER ERASER DAY!
19 help Lyle polish teeth	20 NATIONAL HIGH FIVE DAY!	21 Bulldogs Are Beautiful Day!	22 JELLY BEAN DAY!
26 nothing to do all day (yay!!)	27 MORSE CODE DAY!	28 Blueberry Pie Day!	29 ZIPPER DAY!

Name: Winifred Ma
Date: Wednesday

Name: Winifred Malladi-Maraj
Date: Wednesday, November 2nd

GEOGRAPHY TEST – States

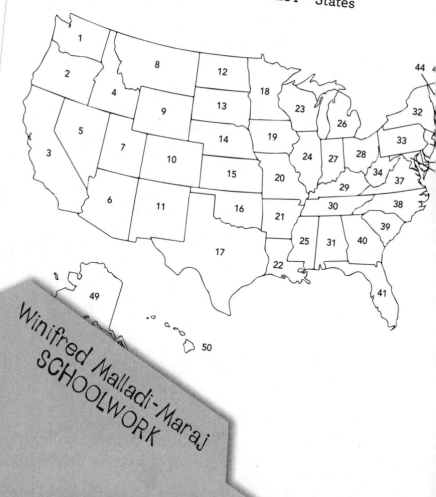

Winifred Malladi-Maraj
SCHOOLWORK

RAPHY TEST – States

31 _____
32 _____ Pennsylvania
33 _____
34 _____
35 _____
36 _____
37 _____
38 _____
39 _____
40 _____
41 _____ Florida
42 _____
43 _____
44 _____
44 _____

45 _____
46 _____
47 _____
48 _____
49 _____
50 _____

5 _____
24 _____
25 _____
26 _____
27 _____
28 _____
29 _____
30 _____

Winnie, Please see me after class. — Mr. B

Mr. B— I didn't have time to study for the geography test because yesterday was Vinegar Day, but I did do some science! Here is a cool science experiment I learned:

HOW TO MAKE AN EGG BOUNCE

You will need:
1 hard-boiled egg
lots of white vinegar
a large bowl

What to do:
#1. Soak the egg in the vinegar for a long time, about three days. Make sure it is a hard-boiled egg!!! Otherwise it won't work.

#2. Rinse the shell off the egg under cold water. It will come off really really easily.

#3. Bounce the egg on the table or floor. It's bounces really high like a rubber ball! Isn't that cool??

Name: Winifred Malladi-Maraj
Date: Monday, February 1ˢᵗ

Winnie, is everything OK? – Mr. B

MATH TEST – Word problems

1. Albert had $200 to spend on new clothes. He bought two shirts for $35.50 each, a pair of pants for $79.99, and a $16.50 pair of shoes. How much money did Albert have left over?

~~35.50~~ ✗

~~200.79~~

Mr. B—I didn't have time to study for this test because it was Backwards Day. But I've been working on my backwards handwriting. Neat, right?
—Winnie

2. Thomas collected 306 bottle caps in five years. If he continues to collect bottle caps at the same rate, how many bottle caps will he have collected by the end of the sixth year?

Winifred Malladi-Maraj
SCHOOLWORK

...h, and four pears for $0.95

Name: Winifred Mallard ~~M~~

Date: Thursday, April 13th

A BOOK REPORT ABOUT *THE TRUMPET OF THE SWAN*

The Trumpet of the Swan is a book by E. B. White, who wrote some other books, too. *The Trumpet of the Swan* is about a swan who gets a trumpet. 🌀

Trumpets are a good way to make music, and so is being in a barbershop quartet. Tuesday was Barbershop Quartet Day. Here are some facts about barbershop quartets:

1. They are always quartets (which means four people!).

2. Each person always sings a different part (like bass, tenor, alto, soprano).

3. A barbershop quartet does not have to perform in a barbershop. They can sing anywhere they want.

That is my book report on *The Trumpet of the Swan*, a book by E. B. White.

🌀 Winnie, I know you didn't have time to read the book before your report, but you should now. It's super good!
— Squizzy

Winnie, let's talk during lunch.
— Mr. B

Grim Grades

1 day before what happened happened

Winnie felt a squirm in her stomach as the rest of her classmates headed to the cafeteria that Thursday afternoon. She stayed behind at her desk, wishing Buttons, the world's greatest cat, were there to snuggle her. She knew that whatever Mr. Benetto wanted to talk to her about wasn't going to be anything good.

Just before the door to Room 5L swung shut, Lyle poked his head back inside to check on her. *You okay?* he asked Winnie with his eyebrows. She gave him a *maybe . . . we'll see* shoulder shrug.

"Winnie," Mr. B said the instant the door was closed. He perched himself on the edge of his desk, which was only one row away from Winnie's—not nearly far enough. "Is everything all right at home?"

Winnie wasn't entirely sure how to answer that question. Technically, everything at home was fine. Her parents were weird, but what was new about that? And everything in her treehouse was even better.

Winnie shrugged.

"I'm asking," Mr. B went on, tapping his fingers on the edge of his desk, "because you've been doing very poorly on all of your assignments and tests, for quite some time now."

"I'm sorry about the book report," Winnie cut in quickly. "I should've spent more time on it. I . . ." The truth was, Winnie *had* had time for the book report, the night before, during what she'd thought was a nothing-special Wednesday in her treehouse. She *could* have read *The Trumpet of the Swan*. She *could* have written the entire book report that night, instead of banging out a few words about barbershop quartets on the library computer during first recess. But Wednesdays were the only days Winnie had to herself. She'd wanted to doodle in her brand-new sketchbook. She'd wanted to snuggle Buttons and fall asleep watching the stars. She had not wanted to read about swans. "I'm sorry," she finished lamely.

Mr. B frowned. "It's not simply the book report," he told her. "You're a smart kid, Winnie. And I've talked to your previous teachers, and I know that you used to receive excellent grades. But this year—"

"I'll try harder," Winnie said quickly. She felt miserable. She wanted Buttons more than ever in that moment, even if it would be weird to snuggle a cat at her desk. "Maybe you could

Winnie, did you just put this part in to brag? (Ha-ha) —Joey

make more of the tests be on Thursdays? Then I'd have lots more time to study."

"I'm just . . . worried about you, Winnie," Mr. B said. "And your parents . . ." His frown grew much deeper. "I've tried to talk to them, but I haven't gotten anywhere."

"Yeah," Winnie said. "They can be, um, difficult."

Mr. B studied her for a moment, like he was trying to figure out everything about her just from her face. Winnie tried to look as normal as possible. Finally, Mr. B clapped his hands together.

"I'm going to be frank with you, Winnie." Winnie sat up a little straighter in her desk. "Your grades are not good."

Winnie allowed herself a little slouch. That news wasn't surprising at all. What with all the time she'd spent celebrating International Tongue Twister Day and Sled Dog Day and Flossing Day, she'd hardly had time to study for a single test all year.

"In fact," Mr. B went on, "you're in serious danger of failing fifth grade."

At that news, Winnie nearly shot out of her desk. *Failing?* she squeaked. *That* was a surprise.

"As a matter of fact, yes," Mr. B said. "Normally this would be a conversation I'd have with your parents, but as I said, they've proved . . . less cooperative than one might like. So I'm telling you, Winnie. We have one more major project coming up before the end of the school year—the local history report.

It's your last chance to boost your grades enough to graduate."

What would happen, Winnie wondered, if she didn't pass fifth grade? Would she be forced to stay in Mr. B's class another year, while all her friends went off to middle school without her? And what if she failed *again* after that? Would she be doomed to repeat fifth grade over and over and over, until she was the oldest kid who'd ever gone to Tulip Street Elementary?

"Winnie?" Mr. B said. "Are you listening?"

Winnie snapped back into the conversation. "Um . . . ," she started, but thankfully Mr. B repeated himself.

"Your local history report," he said. "It's due at the end of the month. That's a little over two weeks from now. If you can manage a good grade on that—I'm talking an A, A-minus, *minimum*—you'll be off to middle school without any further word from me."

"Oh." Winnie gulped. One report. She could do that. One report was no big deal, right? "Okay," she said.

"Good. And, Winnie? Your parents . . . I mean . . ." Mr. B studied Winnie's face again. "Is everything entirely . . . ?"

Winnie decided there was no point trying to explain her parents, so instead she said, "I'll ace the history report. I promise."

"Glad to hear it," Mr. B said, finishing up his face-studying. "I'm expecting something *great*, though, you understand? You'll need to work on it every day until it's due."

"Right," Winnie said. "Every day. Sure thing." She tried

not to worry about whether or not that would be possible. There was too much rolling around in her brain already. "Can I go to lunch now?" she asked.

"Of course."

And with that, Winnie left to join her friends in the cafeteria.

To:	alexis.maraj@math-mazing.org; malladivarun@fecalresearch.gov
From:	hector.benetto@tulipstreetelementary.edu
Date:	Thursday, April 13th
Subject:	your daughter's grades

Dear Dr. Maraj and Dr. Malladi,

I've tried numerous times to call each of you with no success in scheduling a meeting; I'm hoping this email with do the trick. It is crucial that the two of you come in to meet with me for a parent-teacher conference regarding your daughter's grades and her future. I cannot stress enough that Winnie is in danger of failing the fifth grade. I've just had a talk with Winnie herself, and I believe that she understands the situation—
I must say I'm deeply concerned that neither of you seem as worried.

Please do be in touch ASAP about a time when we can all meet to discuss this very serious matter.

Sincerely,
Hector Benetto

To: hector.benetto@tulipstreetelementary.edu
From: alexis.maraj@math-mazing.org
Date: Thursday, April 13th
Subject: RE: your daughter's grades

Dear Mr. Benetto,

As I stated on the phone the last four times you called, I'm happy to come into the school to talk about Winifred, but not if you keep inviting her father as well. I do wish you'd stop involving him in these matters. I take Winifred's well-being very seriously, unlike SOME parents I could name.

Best wishes,

Alexis Maraj

To:	hector.benetto@tulipstreetelementary.edu
From:	malladivarun@fecalresearch.gov
Date:	Thursday, April 13th
Subject:	RE: your daughter's grades

Dear Mr. Benetto:

Why do you always insist on addressing Winifred's mother first in all of your correspondence? You do realize that I've won at least six more awards than she has, don't you?

By the way, I need to talk to you about a very exciting opportunity. (Do you know much about bird feces?) I will be awaiting your phone call this afternoon to discuss it.

Dr. Varun Malladi

Artist Vision

1 day before what happened happened

As Winnie made her way to the cafeteria for lunch, she decided not to tell her friends about her conversation with Mr. B. She knew they'd understand (they were very understanding friends), but just at that moment, what Winnie wanted was to forget all about talks with the teacher and local history reports and her weird parents. So she pushed the thoughts to the farthest corner of her mind and focused on happier things.

"Winnie's here!" Lyle called across the cafeteria when Winnie stepped through the double doors. Winnie smiled and scurried over to the fifth-grade table, where she squeezed onto the bench between Squizzy and Greta.

"Finally," Aayush said. "Squizzy wouldn't let us eat the cupcakes till you got here."

"It's *my* birthday," Squizzy replied, tilting the pink crown that Greta had made for her. "We eat cupcakes when I say." Squizzy wrapped one arm around Winnie. "And now that Winnie's here, I say okay!"

"Singing first," Tabitha demanded. And while everyone sang "Happy Birthday" to Squizzy, Winnie turned on her Artist Vision to better observe each of her friends.

Uncle Huck was the person who'd taught Winnie about Artist Vision. Even though Uncle Huck was an architect, which was not technically an artist, he had what he liked to call an "artistic mind," and he said Winnie had one, too. He claimed that the two of them shared an ability to see things in ways that most other people couldn't. (Winnie's mom claimed that Uncle Huck's "artistic mind" was simply Uncle Huck's excuse to live like a slob, but Winnie disagreed.) When Winnie turned on her Artist Vision, it was like the light shifted, just a little, and she could observe things at a new angle—better, deeper, truer.

She observed, for example, the way Squizzy's eyes lit up when Jolee handed her a sparkly green gift bag and the way she ripped through the tissue paper. So Winnie knew that even though Squizzy said, "Oh, you didn't have to get me anything," she was actually thrilled to get a gift. "*Anne of Green Gables*!" Squizzy squealed. "Thanks, Jolee! I've been wanting this one." She began reading right away.

Winnie turned off her Artist Vision and nudged Greta beside her. "Did you . . . ?" she whispered softly, so Squizzy wouldn't hear. (Winnie probably didn't need to whisper, because when Squizzy had her nose buried in a book, she never heard anything else anyway.)

Yep, that's pretty much true. — Squizzy

"These were the ones you wanted, right?" Greta asked, pulling a wad of embroidery thread out of her pocket. Red, yellow, and two shades of orange—Squizzy's favorite colors. "You're so nice to make Squizzy a bracelet for her birthday. I mean, since she's one of your best friends. I mean, it must be super nice to have a best friend."

Winnie was feeling a little guilty about not having finished a super-awesome present for Squizzy's birthday already. But when you only have one treehouse afternoon a week, there's only so much you can squeeze in.

"Thanks," Winnie told Greta. "Here." She handed over half her ham sandwich. Greta was always happy to exchange craft supplies for lunch food, because her dad only ever packed her healthy things she hated, like cucumber-sprout wraps. And so, in between bites of ham sandwich and chocolate cupcakes, Greta taught Winnie how to make a friendship bracelet for Squizzy's birthday present.

While Winnie and Greta worked, Jolee pulled out her Scrabble board. "Your turn today, Lyle!" she announced. Nobody ever beat Jolee at Scrabble, but everyone in Mr. B's class took turns playing her at lunch anyway. If you could score more than fifty points in a game versus Jolee Watson, it was counted as a win for the whole class, that was the rule.

Winnie finished off a row of knots on her friendship

Don't feel bad, Winnie! The bracelet is my favorite! It has all the best colors! I wear it every day!
—Squizzy

✓ Grossest. Lunch. Ever.
—Greta

bracelet. "What now?" she asked Greta, and Greta showed her.

Lyle placed his first tiles on the board. "Eight points!" he declared proudly.

Tabitha, who was keeping score, wrote the numbers on her scrap of paper.

Jolee didn't seem impressed. "Really?" she asked Lyle. "*Teeth*? That's the best word you could come up with?"

"*Teeth* is the best word in the world!" Lyle said. "Except maybe *floss*. But I don't have an *f* yet."

"You wasted two good *e*'s," Jolee told him.

Tabitha began dumping more letters out of the bag to add to Lyle's tray. "Ooh, look!" she said. "You got a *z*. You could spell *lizard*. Don't you think lizards are the coolest pet in the entire world? Don't you think my grandma should get me a lizard for a graduation present?"

Brogan looked up from where he was trying to sneak carrots into his brother's mound of mashed potatoes. "If you do get a lizard," he said to Tabitha, "can me and Logan borrow it to freak people out?"

"Lizards don't freak people out," Tabitha replied. She lined up Lyle's new letters on the tray in front of him. "At least they shouldn't. Lizards are actually very calm animals."

"Do you think we could train it to eat dragonflies?" Logan asked. "Then we could call it a dragon lizard like on *Dragon Destroyers* and freak out *everyone*."

I was doing that so Logan would accidentally eat carrots and barf. Logan <u>hates</u> carrots.
—Brogan
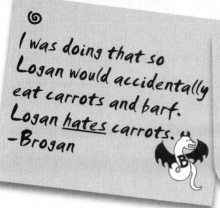

it didn't work though because i was sitting right next to you and i saw!
—logan

✓
LIZARDS RULE!!!!!!!!!
—Tabitha

I'll get you one of these days, Logan, look out!
—Brogan

Winnie, maybe you should explain that <u>Dragon Destroyers</u> is a TV show that Logan and Brogan are obsessed with?

Not everyone who reads this memoir might know that. —Squizzy

who doesn't know about <u>dragon destroy-ers</u>???????
—logan

"*Lizard* would only get you sixteen points," Jolee told Lyle, "unless you placed it on a double letter or something. But there's probably something better you could do with the *z*."

Winnie took a bite of sandwich and finished off another row on her friendship bracelet. "And now?" she asked Greta. But Greta was busy peering over Joey's shoulder at the phone game he was playing, something about bashing blocks. "Greta?" Winnie said. "Um, Greta?"

Finally Greta snapped away from Joey's phone and showed Winnie the next step.

"You could use the *z* to spell *zinc*," Aayush suggested, from the far end of the table. When Lyle looked at him funny, Aayush explained, "Zinc is a chemical element. I was *going* to use it in my science fair experiment and show how when you mix zinc powder with iodine you get this awesome purple smoke; but when I was practicing, my dumb sister added the water too fast and started crying because her stuffed elephant's trunk got disintegrated. She *totally* ruined my experiment, and now my parents are making me do something completely boring for the science fair, like a *volcano* or something, and they want me to spend my allowance to get Ash a new elephant. Can you believe that?"

Winnie turned her Artist Vision back on, watching Aayush. And she observed something very interesting, in the shifted light.

It's called Block Basher. It was cool for a while but then it got sort of boring. I was only playing it because I'd already read the new Blight Boy and Wrench Monkey comic online six times, so I needed something to do.
—Joey

Blight Boy and Wrench Monkey is THE BEST! (Well, except for Joey's comic, but he hadn't started making that one yet.)
—Greta

Aayush's mouth, squinched into a tight, straight line.

His fingers, fiddling with his empty cupcake wrapper as he talked.

Winnie wondered if it was really his science experiment that Aayush was upset about.

"*Zinc* is an even worse word than *lizard*," Jolee told Aayush. "It's only fifteen points."

"Whatever," Aayush grumbled. "My parents are idiots, that's all."

Squizzy must've been turning a page in her book then, because she actually heard what Aayush said. "You think *your* parents are idiots?" she told him. "My parents are going to take away all my books for the next two weeks, so I can 'bring my grades up.' Can you believe that? I'm grounded from reading! Have you ever heard of such a thing?"

"We're grounded from watching *Dragon Destroyers*," Logan told the table. "Well, not *grounded*, exactly. But we will be if we sneak it again. Kyle's allowed to watch it whenever he wants, just because he's older. I swear our mom and dad think we're babies."

"Sounds about as stupid as my parents," Joey said, looking up from his phone. "I asked for more screen time, and they said no way."

"That does sound stupid," Greta said, her gaze fixed hard on the side of Joey's face.

I _was_ upset about that! (But maybe Winnie is right that I _was_ upset about something else, too.)
—Aayush

✓ I can believe it. You failed that math test because you wouldn't stop reading long enough to write your name!
—Lyle

✓ I was reading _Watership Down_ that day! You wouldn't've stopped for math either.
—Squizzy

∥ I was NOT staring at Joey!!! I was watching him playing on his phone!!!
—Greta

"Well, *my* moms," Lyle jumped in, rearranging his tiles on his tray, "don't even care that my cousin ate Squizzy's tooth! They said it was my fault for leaving the display case where Parker could reach it. That toddler's a monster! He'd probably find a way to eat those teeth if I locked them in a safe!"

"Your cousin ate my tooth?" Squizzy asked.

"Yeah, from my display case," Lyle explained.

"Oh," Squizzy replied. And she went back to her reading.

(That last part might be confusing to some people reading this memoir, so it would probably help to explain that Lyle Stenken, future dentist, is obsessed with teeth. He keeps a fancy display case lined with purple velvet, like the kind scientists use to show off weird bugs in museums, full of all his favorites. Most of the teeth in Lyle's display case are from his classmates, because Lyle pays way better than the tooth fairy—six bucks a tooth—and he labels them very carefully. The display case is Lyle's most prized possession.)

"You really don't even care that my cousin ate your tooth?" Lyle asked Squizzy. "It was a *molar*, Squizz. A *molar*! One of my best ones!" But Squizzy was engrossed in her book again.

Winnie offered Lyle a sympathetic frown. He'd already told her about the molar in a note he'd passed to her that morning during Silent Reading, and Winnie didn't need to use Artist Vision to know how upset he was about it.

"At least your cousin's only visiting," Jolee told Lyle.

"With my little sister, it's all 'Oh, Ainslee's *so* cute and *so* funny and *so* . . .' I'm sick of it." Jolee laid down her tiles, working off Lyle's word *teeth* to make *feathery*. "One hundred points," she declared.

Winnie went back to working on her bracelet, looking up every once in a while to observe her friends—the "Tulip Street Ten," as they liked to call themselves. Since Tulip Street Elementary was so small, each grade had only a handful of students, so Winnie had moved from class to class with the exact same kids since kindergarten. And lucky for all of them, the Tulip Street Ten generally got along pretty well.

Next year, Winnie knew, things would be different. Next year, they'd all go off to middle school, where there would be lots of students, in lots of classes. (Well, *hopefully* Winnie would go off to middle school. She pushed the conversation with Mr. B into the farthest corner of her mind.) This was the last year of the Tulip Street Ten. And somehow, like there was a sort of secret pact between them, Winnie could tell that they had all silently vowed to make this year the best one they'd ever had together.

Well, it would definitely turn out to be the *strangest*.

"Winnie?" Lyle asked her.

Winnie snapped out of her thoughts and found Lyle staring at her.

"You okay?" he said. "You look like something's bothering you."

how do you get 100 points on one word??
—logan

The F and the Y were both double-letter squares, so that's 25 pts, and the T was a double-word, which made 50, plus 50 bonus for using all my tiles. 100!!!
—Jolee

Jolee, remind me never to play Scrabble with you ever again.
—Lyle

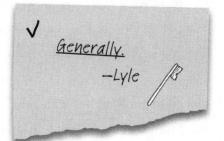

✓ <u>Generally.</u>
—Lyle

For just a moment, Winnie wondered if maybe Lyle had Artist Vision, too.

"I'm . . . ," she began. It would've been so easy to say she was fine. To lie and not bother her friends with her problems at all.

But instead, Winnie tugged at the farthest corner of her mind, pulling out all the thoughts she'd been pushing away, and told her friends the truth. About her grades and her conversation with Mr. B and her weird parents (which they mostly knew about already, being her friends and all). Even Squizzy wrenched her nose out of her book to listen.

"You should tell your parents they're being idiots," Joey suggested when she'd finished her story. "For making you fail fifth grade."

Greta nodded *up-and-down, up-and-down.* "Yeah," she said. "You should. And not just because Joey said it. It's a good idea. Tell your parents you don't want to celebrate any more weird holidays."

Winnie had to admit it was an appealing thought.

"And we can help you with your local history report," Jolee added, rearranging the tiles on her letter tray. "Did you pick a topic yet?"

Winnie was feeling a little better already, just from telling her friends about her problem. "Well, I wanted to write about my treehouse tree," she said. And then she wrinkled her nose.

"But I don't know. Can you write a history report about a tree? It has to be really, really amazing."

"I think it sounds perfect," Squizzy told her. "Plus"—she reached under the lunch table for her backpack, which was always bursting with books—"I've been reading up for *my* report, on the link between our town and that old country, the Republic of Fittizio? And I think this might help you." She hoisted an enormous book onto the table and pushed it toward Winnie, who glanced at the title.

Understanding Embassies and Consulates.

"Read that chapter there," Squizzy said, pointing to a sticking-out bookmark.

(Winnie didn't notice then that there was a folded-up piece of paper half glued to the back cover of book with orange juice.)

(No one else noticed either.)

"Thanks," Winnie said, even though she had no idea what an embassy or a consulate was or how either could possibly help her write a history report about a tree. But if Squizzy said the book would be useful, then Winnie trusted her. She allowed herself a tiny smile and picked up the last of her chocolate cupcake. "I can do it, right?" she asked the group. And when they assured her that she could, Winnie felt more confident than ever. "Yeah," she said. "Everything will be fine."

And just in that moment, Winnie totally believed it.

How to Make an Easy Striped Friendship Bracelet for Your Very Best Friend (or anyone else)

by Greta Regensburger

- four (4) different colors of embroidery thread
- scissors
- a safety pin

What to Do

1. Cut your four colors of embroidery thread about 5–6 feet long. (If you don't have a ruler, stretch the thread as far as you can from arm to arm, and cut there.) Line up all four lengths of thread one next to the other, then fold them in half. Tie a tight knot at the fold, leaving about a half-inch loop at the top.

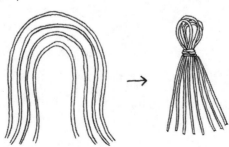

2. Stick a safety pin through the loop, and pin the threads to the knee of your jeans or the back of a chair you can sit in front of, then spread out the threads, alternating the colors evenly.

3. Grab the thread on the far left, and use it to make a 4-shape over the thread just to the right of it.

4. Loop the first thread behind the second one, and pull it through the opening. Pull up and to the right to tighten.

5. Using the same two threads, repeat steps 3–4, so that you've tied the knot twice. When you're done, the first knot should look like this:

6. Keep tying double knots on all six remaining threads, until you have a full row.

7. Grab the thread that's now on the far left, and use it to tie a double knot (just like in steps 3–5) around the thread to its right.

8. Keep tying knots on all six remaining threads, until you have a second full row.

9. Repeat steps 7–8 until the bracelet is long enough to wrap around your wrist. Then tie a tight knot just below the final row, and divide the loose threads into two sections of four threads each. Braid each section until it's about two inches long, and tie a knot at the end of each braid. Cut off any extra thread.

10. Wrap the bracelet around your best friend's wrist and pass one of the braids through the loop, then make a loose knot with the two braids to secure it. You're all done! (I hope your best friend likes the amazing bracelet!)

Plenty of Peaches

1 day before what happened happened

Happy Peach Cobbler Day, Winifred!"

Winnie clutched the giant book Squizzy had loaned her to her chest and looked around her dad's living room. Most normal people who wanted to celebrate Peach Cobbler Day, she thought (which was probably not a whole lot of people), would maybe bake one peach cobbler and leave it at that.

Winnie's dad was definitely *not* a normal person.

"What do you think?" he asked Winnie.

A giant peach-colored banner spanned one whole wall, with HOORAY FOR PEACH COBBLER DAY!!! printed in enormous scrawly letters. (Winnie often wondered if her parents alone were responsible for keeping the local banner-printing shop in business, what with the number of orders they made each week.) From every corner of the room, her dad had strung up round peach balloons, and he'd even added green pipe cleaners, to look like peach stems. There were peach streamers and a peach piñata. On the entry table by the door, peach soda filled a punch bowl large enough to serve forty people, and all around it sat peach-shaped cookies, cupcakes with peach frosting, and several bowls of gummy peaches.

"Very . . . *peachy*," Winnie replied. Then she cleared her throat, gearing up for the serious conversation she knew they needed to have. "Dad, can I talk to you about something? Mr. B told me today that—"

"Ha, *peachy*. That's a good one, Winifred. Well, your mother sent me photos of your Winston Churchill celebration on Monday, and I knew I had to top it. Come in, come in," Winnie's dad urged. "No time to lose! We only have eight hours and"—he checked the clock—"twenty-two minutes until Peach Cobbler Day ends. Wait till you see what's in the kitchen."

Before Winnie could get in another word, her dad scuttled off to the kitchen. Luckily, Buttons (the world's greatest cat) slid through the door behind her then, clearly sensing that he was needed. Winnie set down Squizzy's book and scooped him up, nestling her chin in his soft orange fur. "Good to see you," she whispered. Buttons purred back.

Together, they followed Winnie's dad into the kitchen.

Winnie had seen a lot of weird things in the past year, during her parents' unusual holiday celebrations. The life-size mummy her mom crafted for King Tut Day. The trays and trays of inedible glop her dad had prepared for Moldy Cheese Day. The full-scale re-creation of a post office, for Thank a Mailman

Day. Even a *laser show* for Stuffed Mushroom Day (that had been especially weird). But nothing had prepared Winnie for what she saw when she and Buttons stepped into the kitchen that Thursday.

The floor—the *entire kitchen floor*—was covered with baking pans, each at least five feet wide. Barrels of peaches were crammed onto every counter and tabletop, and what little room remained was crowded with enormous bags of flour and sugar, tubs of butter, and jugs of milk.

"We're making the world's largest cobbler!" her father announced, from his perch on one of the kitchen chairs (there was nowhere else to stand). "Well, sort of." He frowned. "The *largest* was over eleven feet long, and I couldn't find an oven that big on such short notice. But the pizza place across town said if we can get them these pans by ten p.m., they'll bake them in their pizza ovens. And based on sheer volume, our cobbler will definitely trounce the record. I bought these oil drip pans off the auto body shop—brand-new, of course. Smart, right?" He tapped the side of his head. "Bet your mother never would've thought of that. Now help me make the batter. The peaches are already skinned; we just need to slice them."

From the doorway, Winnie cleared her throat, not quite sure what she wanted to say first. "When did you have time to skin all these peaches?" That was what she landed on, peering into the nearest barrel. "There've got to be hundreds of them."

"Seven hundred eighty-two," her father confirmed. "I had my intern at the lab do it. You should've heard him *whine* about it. *'Not even close to my job,'* blah-blah-blah . . ." Balancing on one foot, Winnie's dad reached across to a cupboard. "To work!" he told Winnie, handing her a mixing bowl. "We have *tons* to celebrate."

Winnie shifted Buttons to one arm and took the bowl. "Okay, but, Dad? Before all the celebrating, can I talk to you? About my grades? I need to work on this local history report. It's really important, and I need lots of time to do it. Mr. B said I really have to focus on—"

"Oh, your teacher tried to talk to me about all that." Winnie's father waved the discussion away. "But you can bring your grades up on your mother's days, which I'm sure are dreadfully boring anyway, right? You wouldn't want to miss a celebration like Peach Cobbler Day. Not after I went to all this trouble, just for you." He lifted a barrel and dumped a load of peaches onto a cutting board. Slimy, skinned fruit rolled across the table, bouncing into trays on the floor. "Here, grab that knife, would you?"

"But—"

"Listen, Winifred, I have something I need to talk to *you* about. Some very exciting news."

Winnie nestled her chin deep in Buttons's soft fur. "We'll figure it out," she whispered to him (because she could tell, from

his purrs, that he was worried about her). "About my grades."
Even if she couldn't work on her local history report that afternoon, even if her mom ended up being just as unreasonable
about things as her dad was (which Winnie had to admit was
likely), Winnie always had Wednesdays—there were two left
before the report was due. That wasn't a lot of time to finish
something so important, but Winnie knew she could do it. If
she really tried. If she spent every single second of those two
Wednesdays focusing on nothing but that report.

"Winifred?" her father said, slicing into the first peach. "Did
you hear me? About the exciting news?"

"Oh," Winnie said. "Right." She plopped Buttons down
behind her in the hallway and kicked away one of the enormous cobbler pans so she could pick her way across the floor.
"Is it about peaches?" she asked, joining her dad at the kitchen
table.

"In fact," he replied, sending a peach pit flying as he chopped,
"this news is *even more exciting* than peaches." He puffed out his
chest in suspense, his eyes sparkling. "I have been asked," he told
Winnie, "to join the team researching the potential medicinal
properties of the feces of the lesser prairie chicken."

"Um . . ." Winnie slowly worked through her dad's last
sentence. She knew that *feces* meant "poop," and *lesser prairie
chicken* sounded like a sort of bird. "You're going to study bird
poop?" she asked her dad. And then she remembered that she

was supposed to be excited. "Wow," she added. "I mean . . . congrats."

"Thank you," her dad said. And then he frowned at Winnie, like he thought she might be thinking something she shouldn't be thinking. "You do know the lesser prairie chicken isn't a chicken, right? It's a grouse."

"Oh." Winnie had not known that. What she wanted to ask was why anyone would put the word *chicken* in a bird's name if that bird was not, in fact, a chicken. But instead she simply said, "Cool."

"It *is* cool," her dad agreed. And he smiled a huge smile. "It's a very prestigious position. *Much* more prestigious than any project your mother has worked on." Another peach pit went flying. "We leave for Kansas on June tenth."

From the doorway, Buttons let out an angry *mew!*

"What did you say?" Winnie asked her dad.

"June tenth," her dad repeated, still chopping. "My colleagues will be heading out to set up the facility next month, but I told them we'd need to wait until June tenth to join them. Your teacher seemed awfully insistent that you couldn't leave until the school year ended, even for something as exciting as assisting me in my research. But don't worry, you'll still have plenty of time in the field. We'll be there all summer."

Winnie dodged the peach pit that threatened to take out her left eye.

That does seem like a pretty dumb thing to do.

—Lyle

"All *summer?*" she shrieked. "In *Kansas?* Researching *chicken poop?*" If Winnie spent the whole summer in Kansas, she'd miss Lyle's epic pool party, which he'd agreed to throw on a Wednesday, so Winnie could come. She'd miss Wednesday afternoons at the roller rink with her friends and breezy Wednesday mornings doodling on her treehouse porch. She'd miss Wednesday-night sleepovers at Squizzy's and snuggling in her beanbag bed with Buttons on Wednesday evenings, watching the stars above them.

But her dad didn't seem to care about any of that.

"They're grouse," he corrected her. "Not chickens." He was back to frowning. "And I thought you'd be much more excited about assisting me in my research. Your mother has never offered you such an opportunity. By the end of the summer, you'll be the number-one feces collector on the team."

At that, Buttons couldn't contain himself. "*Meeeeeeeeeeeeeow!*" he growled, leaping into Winnie's arms. Winnie did her best to comfort him, but she was feeling pretty upset herself. "Dad," she said, as calmly as she could, "can't we just talk for one sec—"

That's when her dad's cell phone started to ring, cutting Winnie off. The ringtone was the Wicked Witch theme from *The Wizard of Oz.*

"What on earth does your *mother* want?" Winnie's dad asked, snatching the phone from under a sack of flour. White powder puffed across the kitchen. "Alexis," Winnie's dad snarled

into the phone, "I wish you wouldn't call during my day with— No, Alexis, I do *not* think— No, honestly, I was *not* trying to—". And then he paused. He glanced at Winnie and Buttons, who were now encrusted in a thin layer of flour. "Actually," he said slowly, "I think that might just work out wonderfully. Would you like to tell her?"

Winnie's dad handed Winnie the phone.

"Hello?" Winnie said. Buttons squirmed in her floury arms, like he just *knew* Winnie's mom wasn't about to say anything good.

"Winifred," her mother said quickly, "don't worry. I've solved the problem."

"The problem?" Winnie asked.

"When your father takes you to Kansas this summer, you'll be missing all of your Sundays, Tuesdays, and Fridays with me. Thirty-seven days in total. You hadn't done the math?"

Winnie didn't tell her mom that she hadn't even *thought* about missing Sundays, Tuesdays, and Fridays. She'd only been worried about Wednesdays. But what she said was, "Oh. That's a lot of days." She darted her eyes toward her dad, who was gleefully tossing peach slices in a bowl. "I guess I can't go after all then. Too bad. I was really looking forward to all that chicken poop."

"Grouse poop," her dad corrected, without looking up from his peaches.

Buttons let out an annoyed *mew!*

"No need to skip it," Winnie's mom said on the other end of the phone. "I've come up with a wonderful alternative. Since you'll be missing thirty-seven of my days this summer, you'll just spend your next thirty-seven *Wednesdays* with me. There are nine before you set off for that dreadfully dull trip to Kansas with your father, which leaves us with twenty-eight to make up for after you start sixth grade. That'll take you all the way into next March. You won't need to spend another Wednesday by yourself in that awful treehouse for nearly a full year. Isn't that wonderful?"

Buttons was leaving floury paw prints all over Winnie's favorite black shirt, as though frantically trying to send her a message. But even without the world's greatest cat to alert her, Winnie knew things were desperate.

"Mom," Winnie said. "*No.* You can't do that." No more Wednesdays for an entire year? Even if somehow, impossibly, Winnie managed to pass fifth grade without her next two days in the treehouse, there was no way she could get through sixth without them. "You *can't.*"

"I don't think you understand, Winifred," her mom replied, clearly not recognizing the misery in her daughter's voice. "It really works out perfectly. And don't tell your father, but there are some *amazing* holidays coming up on Wednesdays. Why, just this next Wednesday is National Garlic Day. I've already found a recipe for garlic ice cream. It will be a lot of work on my part, but you're worth the effort, Winifred. I know you're going to *love* it."

As her mom rattled on about all of the exciting Wednesday holidays they'd now get to enjoy together—Windmill Day, Escargot Day, Lumpy Rug Day—Winnie returned her gaze to her father, whose mound of sliced peaches was quickly growing on the cutting board in front of him. She flicked on her Artist Vision and watched him chop in the shifted light.

The gleeful way he hacked the fruit.

His shoulders back, completely relaxed.

The quiet tune he hummed as he worked.

He hadn't taken in one word she'd said about school. About any of it. He was perfectly happy with his peach cobbler. He'd said the celebration was for Winnie, but it wasn't, not an ounce of it.

"And X-Ray Day, and Square Dancing Day, and Crush a Can Day . . . ," Winnie's mom went on.

Through the phone, Winnie did her best to focus her Artist Vision on her mom. She had to imagine, but the picture was clear.

The broad smile as her mom listed new holidays.

The easy way her fingers tapped the table while she spoke.

Her list of celebration ideas, growing longer by the second.

Winnie's mom had said she was planning things for Winnie,

but Winnie didn't *want* her plan. And her mom wasn't listening to her, either.

"*Me-ow,*" Buttons told Winnie miserably as she hung up the phone. And Winnie couldn't have agreed more.

Late that night, after swallowing down more peach cobbler than should legally be allowed, Winnie tucked herself into her bed in the back bedroom of her father's house. Buttons snuggled himself in beside her, but she could tell just by his purrs that he was unsettled as she was.

"We'll figure something out," she told him. But she didn't really believe it.

In between yawns, Winnie pried open the covers of the enormous book Squizzy had loaned her—*Understanding Embassies and Consulates*—and read the chapter Squizzy had bookmarked. Her brain fuzzy with tiredness and worry, Winnie didn't understand at first what the words meant or what they had to do with her local history report or her treehouse.

But just as she was about to set the book down for good and get some sleep, Winnie noticed something unusual.

A folded-up piece of paper, half glued to the back cover of the book with orange juice.

Winnie peeled the paper free.

It was a letter from Squizzy's dad to the town mayor (who just happened to be Aayush's mom). A letter about Winnie's treehouse. A letter Winnie had never been meant to read. ◉

I still can't believe this all started because of a little orange juice stuck to a letter!
—Aayush

I know! My dad says we're never allowed to drink orange juice in our house ever again.
—Squizzy

Winnie read it.

As she read, a thought began to bloom in Winnie's mind. The thought was small at first, like a seed. But by the time she woke up the next morning, that letter still clutched tight in her hand, the thought had bloomed, huge like a sunflower. And suddenly, Winnie knew precisely what she needed to do.

AN INTRODUCTION TO EMBASSIES AND CONSULATES

(So Simple Even Lyle Stenken Can Understand It!)
by Sonia "Squizzy" Squizzato

WHAT IS AN EMBASSY? WHAT IS A CONSULATE?

An "embassy" is a building where citizens of a foreign country can conduct business. This business may include issuing visas, aiding in trade relationships, and assisting in matters of tourism. A "consulate" is like an embassy, but smaller.

WHERE IS AN EMBASSY OR CONSULATE?

This is a tricky question! The easy answer is that embassies and consulates are typically located in or near important cities of foreign countries. For example, the French Embassy to the U.S. is located in Washington, D.C.

But here is a fun fact! The building and surrounding grounds of an embassy or consulate are considered property of that building's country. So when a person passes through the doors of the French Embassy in Washington, D.C., he is no longer in the United States—he is suddenly in France! That visitor would have to follow the laws of France, *not* the United States.

WHAT HAPPENS TO AN EMBASSY OR CONSULATE WHEN THE COUNTRY IT REPRESENTS NO LONGER EXISTS?

Well, now *that's* an excellent question. I guess you'd have to find an embassy historian to answer that one . . .

Maurizio F. Squizzato

201 E. Landsend Ave.
Glenbrook, PA 19066

April 12th

Mayor Leila Asad
100 Center Square
Glenbrook, PA 19066

Dear Mayor Asad:

This past week, I've been helping my daughter Sonia research information about the Republic of Fittizio for her local history report. As I'm sure you already know, the Republic of Fittizio is the long-extinct country that once built a consulate in our humble town. Sonia was inspired to research the country and its consulate because of the plaque on the trunk of her friend Winnie's treehouse.

On a hunch, I did a bit of digging on my own and discovered that the exact spit of land where Winnie's linden tree was planted was in fact the site of Fittizio's former consulate. Although the consulate was long ago torn to the ground, the tree—planted from a Fittizian seed over 150 years ago—remains.

Now, I'm no lawyer, but it occurs to me that this tree—once a product of the Republic of Fittizio and planted on what was technically Fittizian soil—is most likely still part of the now-defunct Republic of Fittizio. All this makes me wonder if perhaps young Winnie's treehouse might not, technically, reside on U.S. land. I worry it's possible (it's unlikely, of course, but I believe it's *possible*) that when Winnie is inside her treehouse, she might not be living in the United States.

Even if I'm correct in my assumptions, I sincerely doubt that this small technical anomaly will ever amount to anything, but I did want to bring the matter to your attention, just in case my hunch is correct. Is there some course of action we can take to address the issue?

Sincerely,

Maurizio Squizzato

Hey, Lyle-o-dile!

I'M SO GLAD IT'S FRIDAY!!!! Last night was the worst. (I will NEVER eat peach cobbler again as long as I live.)

Just wanted to let you know that I can't help you polish teeth next Wednesday, like we planned. Sorry. ☹

— Winnie Pig

P.S. If you're in a country that doesn't exist anymore, then you get to make up all your own laws for that country, right? Do you think that's how it works?

Winnie,

That doesn't look like a pig. Why does it have whiskers and a fork? Why can't you help me polish teeth? I know you have to work on your history project, but maybe you can come over and I'll polish while you work? Pleeeeeeease?????
My cousin Parker tried to snag my teeth <u>again</u> this morning! I caught him in time, but the teeth SERIOUSLY need to be cleaned now and I was counting on you. (I hate that kid!)

—Lyle

P.S. How can you be in a country that doesn't exist anymore?

Lyle-o-dile with a smile—

It's a guinea pig. Get it, like "Winnie Pig," the guinea pig?? And it was holding a <u>paintbrush</u>. Why would a guinea pig have a fork?

I can't polish teeth because I'll be ~~going nowhere~~ somewhere else. Never mind.

—Winnie Pig in a Wig

P.S. If you need me, leave me a note in the treehouse mailbox, OK?

P.P.S. That stinks about your cousin. ☹

Winnie Pig in a Wig with a Twig—
What do you mean you'll be somewhere else? Where are you going? (Anyway, I should probably stop writing, because I think Mr. B is starting to notice that we're

DETENTION SLIP

Stenken
Last Name

Lyle
First Name

Friday, April 14
Date

5L
Room

Reason   passing notes in class

Hector Benetto
Teacher's Signature

Winnie's Sunflower Thought
the day what happened happened!

That Friday after school, while Lyle was serving his detention, Winnie did not go to her mom's house to celebrate Dolphin Day. That was because of the sunflower thought, which was now so huge in Winnie's mind that all she could do was think it and think it. The more she thought it, the bigger it grew.

Here's what Winnie was thinking:

1. If her treehouse wasn't part of the United States, then when Winnie was inside it, she didn't have to follow any of the *laws* of the United States—laws like you have to do what your parents say, especially if your parents are acting like major weirdos and driving you nuts and making you fail fifth grade.

2. If her treehouse was part of the Republic of Fittizio, then when Winnie was inside it, she got to follow the laws of *that* country.

I think everyone should know that I'm such a good friend that I TRIED TO EAT THE NOTE SO Winnie wouldn't get in trouble, too. Even though paper is bad for your digestive system AND your teeth. —Lyle

You've told us this a thousand times, Lyle. We're all super impressed.

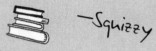

—Squizzy

3. If the Republic of Fittizio didn't exist anymore, then it didn't have any laws anymore, either.

4. So, if Winnie was in her treehouse (which was in the Republic of Fittizio), then she could make up her *own* laws. Laws like she didn't have to come down ever, not unless she wanted to, no matter what anyone else said, even her parents.

Winnie didn't tell anyone about her sunflower thought—not even Lyle or Squizzy or Uncle Huck—because she didn't want anyone to try to stop her from doing what she was thinking about doing. Instead, Winnie slipped a note under her mom's front door, stapled to a copy of Mr. Squizzato's letter to the mayor. Then she crossed to her dad's house and slipped the exact same note under his door. And then she made her way to her treehouse.

Dear Parents,
If you need me I'll be in my treehouse, which as it turns out is its own country, so you can't make me come out unless I want to.
Love,
Winnie

After delivering her two letters, Winnie marched directly to her treehouse. She stuck one foot on the bottom rung of the rope ladder and hoisted herself up, rubbing the bronze plaque that read PLANTED BY THE REPUBLIC OF FITTIZIO for good luck. When she reached the trapdoor, Winnie spun the combination and let herself inside.

And after that, Winnie didn't come down for a long, long time.

Part II

How It All Happened

Talking Through the Window
the afternoon what happened happened!

Winnie figured it wouldn't take long for her parents to do something weird, and as it turned out, she was right. Just about four o'clock, Winnie heard, out the south-facing window of her treehouse, the back door of her dad's house creak open. She saw her dad storming across his back lawn, toward the thick patch of dirt that circled the linden tree. Winnie's note was crumpled in his hand.

Not three seconds later, through her north-facing window, Winnie heard her mom's back door creak open. And Winnie watched as her mom stormed toward the treehouse, clutching her own copy of Winnie's note.

"*Winifred!*" her parents hollered, at exactly the same time.

"You get down here this instant!" her dad shouted.

"I need to talk— Is that your *father*?" Winnie's mom exclaimed.

"What's your *mother* doing here?" Winnie's dad bellowed,

craning his neck to get a better look around the linden's trunk. "Winifred, please tell your mother to go home. I need to talk to you before she does."

"No, Winifred, *I* need to talk to you first!"

Winnie sat perched on the edge of her daybed, staring at the cat door in the treehouse wall, willing Buttons to figure out where she was and come find her. And because Buttons was the world's greatest cat, he sensed what she needed and popped inside the treehouse. Winnie had never been quite so happy to see him.

Once Buttons was comfortably snuggled in her arms, Winnie stood up.

"I'm not coming down," she told her parents out the open windows. "I have a local history report to work on. And also, I don't want to. You can both go home now."

Buttons's purr let Winnie know she had made some excellent points.

"What do you mean you don't want to come down?" Winnie's mom called back, from the northern side of the treehouse. "It's Dolphin Day! Do you realize how much preparation I put into our celebration? I transformed the entire den into an echolocation chamber, just for you."

From the southern side of the treehouse, Winnie's dad snorted. "*Echolocation,*" he said. "Do you know what I've been planning for Rubber Eraser Day tomorrow? Let's just say I've ordered some truly massive rolls of butcher paper. There will be a *lot* of erasing."

"I'd like to erase *you*," Winnie's mom muttered.

"Mom!" Winnie shouted. "Dad! Sheesh! Will you just . . . *stop it*? You're being ridiculous. Both of you."

"*Meow!*" Buttons agreed.

To Winnie's surprise, both of her parents were silent after that. For a moment, Winnie thought she might have hurt their feelings, calling them ridiculous and everything. (She wasn't sure if she felt bad about it or not.)

"You really don't want to come down?" her dad said at last. "Not even for *our* day tomorrow?"

"Nope," Winnie said. She made her voice steady, clear. Buttons pressed his wet nose into the crook of her elbow, for support.

"Well," her mom said slowly. "I guess that's okay."

Winnie hadn't expected that. "It is?" she asked.

"Sure," her mom replied. "I mean, I don't love the idea of you missing your day with me, especially after all the hard work I've put into making a special celebration for you. But I suppose it's fine, as long as you miss your father's day tomorrow, too. That way, everything's still even. That's what's important."

"That does seem reasonable," Winnie's father put in, from his side of the tree trunk.

And that, *that* made Winnie mad.

I told Winnie she
should've said "idiots."
—Joey

"No!" Winnie shouted. She squeezed Buttons tighter. She could tell he was mad, too. "*That's* the problem!" This mess had all started, Winnie realized, when her parents had begun insisting that everything be exactly even between them, all the time. "I don't *care* about even!"

"Oh, now you're just being silly," Winnie's dad said. "Of *course* you care about evenness."

"Winifred, dear," her mom said—and her voice was extra calm, the way you'd try to reason with a fussy toddler who didn't want a bath—"you just let us know when you come to your senses, all right, honey? Well, let *me* know first, obviously, since it's my day you're missing today."

"Wait, why should she talk to *you* first?" Winnie's dad demanded. "She should come to *me* first, since she clearly doesn't want to talk to you to begin—"

"Dad!" Winnie shouted again. "Mom! I don't care *who's* first! And *I'm* not the one who needs to come to my senses!" ("*Mew!*" Buttons added.) "In fact"—a thought popped into Winnie's head just that second, and she liked it at once—"if you guys want me to come down, you have to come up here together, both of you, at the same time, and talk to me."

"Together?" her mom snapped. "With your *father*? Why, I—"

"I've never heard such nonsense!" her dad boomed. "I

think you ought to stay in that treehouse for a while and con-template what you're saying."

"Sounds good to me!" Winnie called back, because it did. It sounded good to Buttons, too; Winnie could tell by his satis-fied snuggles. "And you should both probably leave now, be-cause you're not in America anymore, you know, and that's trespassing." Winnie wasn't totally sure about that last part, but it sounded right.

"Very well then, young lady," her mom said. "I'm leaving."

"Me too," her dad said.

"Fine!" Winnie told them.

"Fine!" they both called back.

And with that, Winnie's parents stomped off the circular patch of dirt at the base of the linden tree, and onto their own lawns. Winnie's mom opened the door to her den. Winnie's dad opened the door to his kitchen.

Slam! went both doors at once.

Buttons gave Winnie a little purr of victory.

She smiled at him. "How about some Froot Loops?" she asked.

Winnie ate four bowls of Froot Loops for dinner that night and gave Buttons all the leftover milk. They worked on Winnie's local history report together and felt very happy with the progress they were making. Winnie even snuck in a little doodling time, occasionally turning her eyes east, watching the curtains of Uncle Huck's windows flutter in the breeze, one block away.

When the sky outside grew dark and the air grew still, Winnie and Buttons tucked themselves under the soft, ratty quilt on top of the beanbag bed in the upstairs loft. And together they gazed out the skylight above them, watching the leaves and the stars and the world, keeping each other company in comfortable quiet.

Maybe, Winnie thought as she drifted off to sleep, everything would work out just perfectly after all.

To:	hector.benetto@tulipstreetelementary.edu
CC:	alexis.maraj@math-mazing.org
From:	malladivarun@fecalresearch.gov
Date:	Saturday, April 15th
Subject:	Winifred's future absences

Mr. Benetto:

This email is to inform you that my daughter, Winifred, is not likely to attend school on Monday. In fact, it is possible that she will be absent for several days or even weeks to come. Please be assured that she is the model of good health; however, Winifred has decided to live inside her treehouse. (I am attaching here a letter from one Mr. Maurizio Squizzato about the legality of the situation.)

Dr. Varun Malladi

P.S. I would like it noted that I sent you an email concerning this predicament before Winifred's mother did.

ATTACHMENT: mauriziosquizzatosletter.pdf

To: ERamundo@glenbrookpolicedept.pa.us.gov
From: hector.benetto@tulipstreetelementary.edu
Date: Saturday, April 15th
Subject: FWD: Winifred's future absences

Dear Chief Ramundo,

Thank you for speaking with me on the phone earlier. As discussed, I'm forwarding the email I received from Winifred Malladi-Maraj's father this afternoon, including the attachment of the letter about the legal implications of Winnie's treehouse. As you and your team investigate further, please do keep Principal Brandon and myself informed about what, if anything, we can or should do to resolve the issue as soon as possible. I do hate the idea of that poor girl staying all by herself up in that tree.

Sincerely,
Hector Benetto

P.S. I will be sending you and your wife a separate email later in the week about Joey's missing homework assignments.

ATTACHMENT: mauriziosquizzatosletter.pdf

A Stupendous Slumber Party

2 days after what happened happened

When Winnie woke up Sunday morning, with the mid-April sun shining a bright wedge onto her face and Buttons purring in her ear, she was happier than she ever remembered feeling. Her parents hadn't tried to come talk to her once the day before (which had been surprising, but nice, too), and she'd made a good dent in her local history report. Winnie didn't have anywhere to be or any weird holidays to celebrate. She was all alone in a country that was just hers, and she was happy.

Knock-knock-knock!

At first Winnie thought the pounding on the trapdoor must be her parents, coming together to talk to her at last. So she didn't exactly jump out of her beanbag bed to answer—not until she heard the voices on the other side.

"Winnie!" Lyle called. "It's me! Can I come up?"

"Me too?" shouted Squizzy.

Winnie leapt down the loft stairs two at a time, with Buttons right behind her. Still in her blue polka-dot pajamas, Winnie spun open the lock as quickly as she could. "I can't believe you guys are here!" she squealed, as her two best friends popped through the trapdoor entrance one after the other. "How did you know where I was?"

Squizzy dumped a bulging backpack on the floor. "My dad's been on the phone since six this morning with Mayor Asad," Squizzy told Winnie. "And I'm a good eavesdropper. Especially when I'm grounded from reading."

"As soon as Squizz told me what you did," Lyle said to Winnie, "I said we had to come. Not that I was too sad to get away from my tooth-eating cousin. I can't believe this is your own country!" Lyle spread his arms wide, and his own enormous backpack thumped to the floor. "You are so smart. This is so cool!"

Buttons meowed in agreement, then took it upon himself to inspect the bags Lyle and Squizzy had brought.

"It is pretty cool," Winnie agreed, a smile working its way onto her face. "I've been doing lots of good work on my local history re—"

"Buttons, no!" Squizzy shouted when she spotted the cat nudging open her backpack zipper with his nose. "Those peanut butter crackers aren't for you!" She snatched her backpack off the floor.

"You guys brought me snacks?" Winnie asked, suddenly appreciating her two best friends even more.

"Well," Squizzy said, piling the contents of her backpack on Winnie's kitchen table. Peanut butter crackers, granola bars, potato chips . . . and books. Lots and lots of books. "The snacks are for everybody."

"Everybody?" Winnie asked.

"We called the whole gang," Lyle said, dumping out his own backpack. Sugar-free hot cocoa. Sugar-free gum. Celery sticks and carrot sticks and packs and packs of dental floss. "They should be here any minute." And before Winnie had even a second to process what he meant, Lyle pulled out his precious velvet-lined tooth case. "Where should I hang this?" he asked. "By the window maybe, where it'll get the best light?"

Winnie blinked once. Then twice. "You . . . you guys want to stay?" she said. "Here?"

"In the Republic of Winnizio?" Squizzy asked, and Winnie had to laugh at the new name for her treehouse. "Of course! You get to make up all your own laws, right? Like how a person can read as much as she wants?"

Lyle polished a scuff from his display case with the elbow of his shirt. "And how toddlers should be forbidden to vandalize teeth?"

"Well . . . ," Winnie said slowly, thinking things over. "I guess. Yeah, I mean . . ." It had never occurred to her that anyone else might want to join her in the treehouse. It had never occurred to her that her friends might have their own reasons for leaving the country.

Knock-knock-knock!

"Winnie?" came a voice. It was Aayush. "Are you in there? It's me! Squizzy and Lyle said I could stay with you until my parents change their minds about my science project."

"And me!" That voice sounded like Logan's. "Me and Brogan aren't coming down until we get to watch *Dragon Destroyers* just like Kyle!"

"I'm here, too!" Winnie was pretty sure that voice belonged to Joey. "I had to sneak out when my dad wasn't looking. I told him I need more screen time, but he won't listen."

"I think Joey's so brave for sneaking out!" That was obviously Greta. "And I want to live in the treehouse, too!"

When Winnie whipped back the trapdoor again, she found all of her remaining classmates from Tulip Street Elementary, stacked like blocks, one on top of the other on the treehouse ladder.

"We want to join your country!" Tabitha called up.

Her friends, Winnie noticed, were all carrying backpacks stuffed to bursting. She glanced at Squizzy and Lyle, not quite sure what to make of everything.

It was in that moment that Lyle lifted his gaze from his display case and looked at Winnie, very serious. "Is it okay if we join you, Winnie?" he asked. "I mean, we all have reasons for wanting to be here, too, but it's up to you, obviously. It's your treehouse. Whatever you say is fine."

Squizzy nodded from her spot on the floor, even though her

nose was already deep in her copy of *Anne of Avonlea*. "Whatever you say!" she agreed.

Winnie looked at her two best friends, sitting there in her treehouse, and she looked down at her seven other classmates, squeezed onto her treehouse ladder, and she knew immediately what her answer would be.

"Come on up!" she shouted to the others. After all, why wouldn't she want the Tulip Street Ten to join her in her very own country? Buttons purred in agreement.

It turned out that having ten kids in a treehouse, without any adults to tell them what to do, was even better than Winnie could have imagined. It was like being at the world's most stupendous slumber party, where everyone got to spend the day doing exactly what they wanted to do most.

Joey played games on his phone—as many as he felt like, with no limit on screen time—until the battery died. (He hadn't thought to bring the charger, but that turned out to be okay, because his dad kept calling and shouting at him to come down this second, and that was getting old.) After that he joined the others in any game they could dream up—charades and G.H.O.S.T. and twenty questions and Act Out Your Favorite Scene from *Dragon Destroyers*. (Logan and Brogan made up that last one.)

They ran relay races, jumping from the loft onto the couch, and no one even broke an arm or anything.

Anne of Avonlea is the sequel to Anne of Green Gables, and it's SO GOOD!
—Squizzy

✓

Well, not <u>then</u>.
—Brogan

They debated whether or not they should throw all the water balloons Brogan and Logan had brought out the window at the parents gathering outside, who were blocked from entering the treehouse by a growing police force. But Logan and Brogan didn't want to use up their whole stash at once, so in the end they threw only half.

Greta taught everyone how to make friendship bracelets. Tabitha talked about the lizard she wanted, and Aayush talked about his dream experiment for the science fair. Winnie worked on her local history report in her loft, with the cheerful sounds of her friends drifting up from the floor below. And when she'd done as much work as she wanted, she climbed down the steps to join them, knowing she could get right back to work the next day.

They sang songs. Squizzy read books. Lyle polished his tooth collection. Greta followed Joey around everywhere. Jolee played travel Scrabble with anyone who'd join her. Everyone paid lots of attention to Buttons, giving him more snuggles and smooches than he'd had in a long time. And when he wanted to curl up and be alone, they let him do that, too.

They ate the last of Winnie's Froot Loops for dinner and peanut butter crackers and celery and carrots. Afterward, Lyle lectured them all about proper flossing technique. (Luckily, he'd brought enough dental floss for everyone.)

And even though Winnie found herself glancing out the

@ A red ackie!!! I'd name it
"Ackie." Isn't that a good
name for a lizard?
—Tabitha

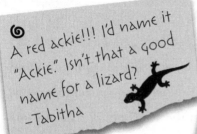

✔
It's all about density,
and how elevation can
affect the

✔ Snooze-fest,
Aayush!
—Squizzy

= I did not! We were
just going to all the
same places!
—Greta

✗
You know we all thought
that was boring, right,
Lyle? —Squizzy

✗
No way that was boring.
Teeth are the most exciting
thing there is! —Lyle

windows every once in a while, watching to see if her parents would come try to talk to her, she was glad they didn't. She'd have hated to leave the world's most stupendous slumber party.

As the sun began to set and the swarm of parents outside grew louder and angrier, the Tulip Street Ten got to the very important work of writing up a list of demands, so everyone back on U.S. soil would know exactly what it would take to get them to leave the Republic of Winnizio for good—although at that point, it was hard to imagine they'd ever want to.

How to Floss Your Teeth the Right Way

A Very Exciting Instruction Manual

(with tooth-friendly fun facts!)

by Lyle Stenken

Step #1

Wind about a foot-and-a-half of floss around your two middle fingers, with a couple inches stretched between your hands. Pull the floss tight, but not so tight you cut off circulation to your fingers. Fingers aren't as cool as teeth, but they're still important.

Fun Fact #1:

Teeth can be valuable for more than just chewing! A molar of John Lennon's, that dude from the Beatles, sold for $31,000! Isaac Newton's sold for even more! (Someone made it into a ring. Like, one that you can wear.)

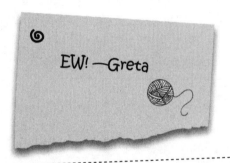

EW! —Greta

Step #2

Insert the stretched floss between two of your teeth and slide it up and down a little. Be gentle! Gums are delicate.

Fun Fact #2:

The Historical Dental Museum in Philadelphia has a necklace made from 357 teeth! An old-timey dentist named Painless Parker (that was his real name—he changed it from Edgar) pulled them all himself. Painless Parker traveled around the country pulling people's rotten teeth for fifty cents a tooth, while a marching band played next to the dental chair.

Step #3

Curve the floss all the way around the base of your tooth, getting underneath the gum line. That's where nasty bacteria like to hide.

Fun Fact #3:

Dental floss isn't only good for oral hygiene! In 1994, an inmate escaped a West Virginia prison by braiding dental floss into a rope and using it to climb an eighteen-foot wall!

Step #4

Stretch a new section of floss between your fingers, and floss some more teeth! (This step is super important! If you use the same section of floss for each tooth, you're just spreading the bacteria around, which is gross.)

Fun Fact #4:

Before we had modern dental care, there were some pretty strange ideas about how to cure toothaches. In medieval Germany, people would kiss donkeys to try to get rid of the pain! And in Ancient Rome, they thought it would help to catch a frog under a full moon and spit in its mouth!

EW! —Greta

✓

I'd rather spit in a
frog's mouth than go
to the dentist.
            —Brogan

TRANSCRIPT

The following is what was said on the Channel 10 Action News special report that aired the night of Sunday, April 16th—the same day the Tulip Street Ten joined Winnie in her treehouse.

Amanda Howard, Channel 10 Action News Correspondent: This is Amanda Howard, live from the site of a local treehouse, where a girl named Gwendolyn Magadi-Mirage, or "Gwinnie," has taken up residence with the rest of her classmates. 🌀

Frank Quijata, Channel 10 Action News Cameraman: [voice heard off camera] Psst! Psst, Amanda! That's not the girl's name. It's Win—

Amanda Howard: Frankie, quiet, we're live! People can hear you! [smiles to camera] As I was saying, little Gwinnie and her friends have decided to live in this treehouse. And there's nothing anyone can do to stop them. You see, this tree was planted years ago on the site of a consulate, so now the treehouse belongs to the country of Fabrizio.

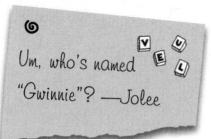

Um, who's named "Gwinnie"? —Jolee

Frank Quijata: [voice heard off camera] Psst! Amanda! It's called the Repub—

Amanda Howard: [very angry] Frankie, if you think you can do my job, just let me know, I'll be happy to hold the camera. [smiles again] I have with me Edward Ragu, the local police chief. He's also the father of one of the little kids in the treehouse, Josie Ragu. Mr. Ragu, what are you doing to get these children down?

Police Chief Ramundo: Uh, thanks, Amanda. Uh, well, to be honest, there isn't a whole lot we can do to remove the kids at the moment. A lot of smart folks are looking into the situation, but according to our best intel, the law seems clear. As long as the children are in the treehouse, they're not on American soil, so they're not bound by American laws. Which means they can stay up there pretty much as long as they want and do pretty much whatever they feel like. [clears throat] Not that my team and I aren't developing some, uh, tactics to try to urge them down more quickly.

Ha-ha, I'm totally going to call my dad that now! —Joey

✓

Ha-ha, Josie!! ☺ —Brogan

Amanda Howard: I see. But aren't you terribly worried, as a parent, that your delicate little girl Josie is up there without you? Don't you worry she might get into some sort of trouble?

Police Chief Ramundo: Well, Josie—I mean, Joey, my son—he's a very good kid. He might spend far too much time on that phone of his, but [clears throat again] . . . Anyway, yes, of course I worry. I think all the parents here are worried about their kids.

[The camera zooms out to show lots of other parents milling about on the grass. There are several other reporters and news crews as well, along with a handful of bystanders filming with their phones. Policemen are busy setting up barricades around the tree. Winnie's mother and father are nowhere to be seen.]

Police Chief Ramundo: But my job is to uphold the law, even if I don't always agree with the law itself. Right now we're mainly concerned with keeping the children safe inside that treehouse, which means not allowing anyone through unless the children say it's okay.

Amanda Howard: You heard that here, folks. Not even the head of police can get these tiny tots out of their tree. For Channel Ten Action News, this is Amanda Howard, signing ou— Oh! Frankie! Zoom in there! Folks, it looks like the kids are lowering something on their mailbox platform. It looks like . . . a letter! Frankie, you got it? Can you see it, Frankie? Let's get closer! [talking to camera, while rushing nearer to the treehouse] It seems these desperate kiddos are trying to communicate with us. What could they possibly be trying to—?

[Amanda's head grows blurry as she gets too close to the camera. She soon collides with it. There is a shriek, then the feed cuts out.]

THE <u>VERY SERIOUS</u> DEMANDS OF THE
TULIP STREET TEN!!

(Hey, everybody down there! We're not coming out of this treehouse, ever, until we get every single thing on this list. The stuff about the teeth is extra important!)

Here's what we ~~want~~ demand:

<u>Lyle</u>: If anyone messes with our most prized possessions (like valuable TEETH in an expensive display case!), then that person has to find somewhere else to visit and can't stay in our house anymore, even if they are just a toddler (STOP EATING MY STUFF, PARKER!!!!!!!!!!!!!!!!!). Also I would like a special shelf for my display case, where no one can get it but me. And if we ever buy a new house there should be a whole ROOM to display my teeth. I'm serious!!

<u>Aayush</u>: All of us get to work on whatever experiments we want for the science fair, even if we did accidentally burn the trunk of Ash's stuffed elephant, which by the way she never cared about before even if she's totally crying and acting all bothered about it now.

<u>Tabitha</u>: A pet lizard for a graduation present. A red ackie, to be exact! Lizards are NOT gross, Grandma!

<u>Joey</u>: ~~More~~ Unlimited screen time.

<u>Greta</u>: We all get to go to Joey's whenever we want, to play phone games and read comic books. (Joey has a really good comic book collection!)

<u>Brogan</u>: We get to watch <u>Dragon Destroyers</u>, which is totally not that violent.

<u>logan</u>: what brogan said. kyle gets to watch the show, and we're just as mature as he is! and if anyone says we're not, we have tons of water balloons to prove them wrong.

<u>Squizzy</u>: As much time as we want to read, no matter what our grades are. NO MORE GETTING GROUNDED FOR READING!

<u>Jolee</u>: Our parents have to play Scrabble with us whenever we want, even if our annoying little sisters have gymnastics or swimming or piano or are just "being cute" or whatever. And if we think our little sisters are being annoying, we get to lock them in their rooms.

<u>Winnie</u>: My mom and dad have to come to the treehouse together and talk to me at the same time.

Winnie, are you sure this is all you want? You can ask for <u>anything</u>.

That's it.

A Stack of Surprises

3 days after what happened happened

Guys!" Aayush called from the east-facing window first thing Monday morning, when Winnie was brushing her teeth. "You have to see this!"

Winnie rushed to the window, her toothbrush wedged in her mouth.

"Wow," she said, around her toothpasty spit.

Her parents' two lawns were completely covered—jam-packed—with parents and reporters and random people milling around. The thick patch of dirt that circled the linden tree was still surrounded by barricades, manned by Glenbrook's local police force. ("Hi, Dad!" Joey called down to Police Chief Ramundo, when he joined Winnie at the window. Joey's dad offered a weary wave.) Even beyond Winnie's parents' homes, Circle Road was bursting with vehicles and news crews.

"You think all these people are here because of us?" Brogan asked, rubbing his eyes at the crowd below.

"Nah," Logan teased. "They're probably watching the kids in the treehouse next door."

"There is no treehouse next door," Tabitha chimed in.

"Hey, Winnie," Aayush interrupted. "I think someone's trying to get your attention."

"Uncle Huck!" Winnie hollered, spotting her uncle in the crowd. "Hey!" She waved wildly, leaning out over the window-sill. Down below, the news reporters clamored to get a good shot of her.

"Can I come up?" Uncle Huck shouted back. "The police say no one can visit without an invitation!"

"Of course!" Winnie stuck her hands on either side of her mouth, making sure Joey's dad heard her loud and clear. "Let him up!"

Police Chief Ramundo shifted one arm of the barricade, and Uncle Huck made his way through to the rope ladder, as cameras continued to flash.

"Did you really just invite a *grown-up* into our treehouse?" Logan asked Winnie, tugging closed the curtains.

"Uncle Huck's not a grown-up," Lyle informed Logan, as he poured himself a bowl of sugar-free cereal at the sink. "He's *Uncle Huck*. And anyway, it's Winnie's treehouse."

Knock-knock-knock!

Winnie raced to the trapdoor and spun the lock, then pulled the door back to let in her uncle. As soon as Uncle Huck

Tabitha, you know
Logan was making
a joke, right?
—Squizzy

I don't get it.
—Tabitha

climbed inside, Winnie tackled with him with a hug. He tackle-hugged her right back.

Uncle Huck was Winnie's mom's brother and Winnie's dad's best friend from college. He was the reason Winnie's parents had met in the first place, although they both liked him so much they tried not to hold it against him. Uncle Huck was hands down Winnie's favorite relative. He'd been there for every one of her birthday parties, he volunteered for school field trips, and, of course, he'd built the treehouse.

"It's good to see you, Winnie," Uncle Huck said, taking in the scene around him. The sleeping bags scrunched into every corner. The dirty dishes piled in the sink. The art supplies and books and empty dental-floss containers littering the floor. "Looks like you guys are having a good time up here."

Winnie smiled. "You want to meet everyone?" she asked.

"The famous Treehouse Ten?" And when Winnie looked confused, he explained, "That's the name the world has given you."

"The world?" Jolee asked, peering down from the loft.

Uncle Huck nodded seriously. "Didn't you know? You all have gotten pretty famous overnight. Blogs and newspapers all over the world are picking up the story of the 'Treehouse Ten.' 'Kids with a cause'—that's what they're saying about you. You want to see?" He pulled his phone from his pocket.

"*Do* I?" Joey exclaimed, snatching the device from Uncle

Huck's hand. (Secretly, Winnie thought Joey was just glad to see a working phone again.) Immediately he got online to discover what Uncle Huck was talking about. The others gathered around to discover, too.

Video after video, that's what they discovered. Post after post. Tweet after tweet. Hundreds of them. Thousands of them. All about the Treehouse Ten.

"We really are famous," Lyle said, stunned.

Everyone, it seemed, had an opinion about Winnie and her friends.

Some folks—grown-ups, mainly—were horrified by the idea of children living in their own country, with nothing to stop them from doing whatever they wanted. They said Winnie and her friends were a bunch of "rabble-rousers." Around the globe, adults seemed to agree that kids were kids and that they had to listen to their parents' rules, no matter what those rules were. The Treehouse Ten, these adults said, couldn't just run off and hide in a treehouse until they got whatever silly thing they demanded.

Other folks—kids mainly—saw the Treehouse Ten as heros, standing up for what they believed in and fighting back against the "cruel power of parental injustice." From every corner of the planet, children were cheering on the Treehouse Ten, urging them to stay in the linden tree as long as they could. "For kids everywhere!" they wrote.

what a dumb grown-up thing to say.
—logan

Our demands were <u>NOT</u> silly!
—Lyle

Until that moment, Winnie had never thought of herself as either a rabble-rouser *or* a hero. She'd just been a girl in a treehouse.

As Joey and the others hunkered over the phone, Uncle Huck pulled Winnie away from the group to talk to her.

"How are you doing?" he asked. "I mean, really?"

Winnie turned on her Artist Vision, observing her uncle Huck in the shifted light.

His hands in his pockets.

His mouth a thin line of worry.

His eyes lit up with the slightest twinkle.

Uncle Huck was concerned about her, Winnie observed. But he was proud of her, too.

"I'm good," she told him. "Really." And then she stuck her hands in her own pockets. "Have you, um, talked to Mom and Dad?" she asked.

Uncle Huck plopped down in one of the chairs by the kitchen table and let out a deep sigh.

"What did they do now?" Winnie said.

There was a quiet *thump*ing of cat paws as Buttons hopped down from the loft above, just roused from his morning snooze. He made his way over to Uncle Huck, to receive snuggling. Uncle Huck pulled Buttons into his lap and scratched under his kitty chin.

"Your dad," Uncle Huck said slowly, "wanted to know if

you'd left your note under your mom's door before you left the one under his." Buttons purred as Uncle Huck scratched a little harder. "And your mom just wanted me to confirm that the two of them had an equal number of trespassers on their lawns."

Winnie couldn't help it. She snorted. Uncle Huck allowed himself a snort of his own. But he soon got serious again. "You know I'm always here for you, Winnie. Whatever you need. Any time of day." He jerked his chin toward the window that faced his house. "I'm only a zip line away."

"Thanks," Winnie said. And she meant it. "But I don't want to leave. Not until my parents do what I asked."

"You mean, your very reasonable request that they agree to come up here together, at the same time, and talk to you like levelheaded adults?" Uncle Huck asked.

For the first time, Winnie worried that maybe *her* demand, more than any of her friends', would be absolutely impossible to achieve. "You think they'll ever do it?" she asked her uncle hopefully.

Uncle Huck thought awhile, scratching away at Buttons's favorite spot. "I think," he said at last, "that you're going to need more Froot Loops." And then the twinkle returned to his eye. "Luckily, I have a good idea where you might find some." He nodded toward the mailbox light on the wall, which Winnie now noticed was glowing red.

"You brought supplies!" Winnie cried.

"Not just me. Take a look."

Sure enough, when Winnie checked the mailbox platform, she found a towering stack of packages. Boxes of all sizes, enough to fill a car trunk. "But who . . . ?" She turned back to her uncle.

"I told you," he said. "You're famous now. The only person allowed past the barricade without an invitation is the mailman, and apparently he's been *very* busy."

Winnie managed to drag her friends away from Uncle Huck's phone long enough to help with the surprise delivery. The group tugged and tugged, and when the tower of heavy boxes at last appeared above the window, Logan hooted with such shock that they nearly lost hold of the rope, sending everything tumbling back down to the ground. "To the Treehouse Ten" was written on the address label of each package, with OVERNIGHT MAIL stamps plastered all over.

"Listen to this," Jolee said, pulling a sheet of paper from the first box. "It's a letter, to us. From some sisters in Tennessee. They wrote, 'Use this stuff to stay up there as long as you can. We're all *rooting* for you!'" Jolee flashed them the note. "They underlined 'rooting' and drew a tree with big roots underneath."

"Did a bunch of strangers really just mail us stuff?" Aayush wondered, unloading the contents of the box. "Isn't that kind of weir— Ooh, Cheetos!"

A bunch of strangers, had, indeed, mailed them stuff. In

fact, dozens of strangers, from all over the world, had sent them things. The Treehouse Ten spent a large chunk of their day opening packages and breaking down boxes and finding space to store all the supplies they'd been given. Some of the things were helpful—blankets, paper plates, cat food. Some were not—squash rackets, a package of green toe socks, and even a dictionary with a broken spine. Winnie and her friends unpacked it all. But Winnie's favorite box was the one from Uncle Huck. It was crammed with Froot Loops and hot cocoa (the kind with the mini marshmallows, Winnie's favorite) and bread and peanut butter, and tons of practical things like toothpaste and toilet paper and hand soap. And buried at the very bottom was a new helmet—turquoise and purple zigzags, much more stylish than her old one—for the zip line.

"It never hurts to be prepared," Uncle Huck explained.

Winnie tucked the zip-line helmet in a cubby of her art station, next to her sketchbook, and when it was time for Uncle Huck to leave, she gave him another fierce hug. She appreciated Uncle Huck's thoughtfulness—although she was certain she'd never need to use the helmet. Why would anyone ever want to leave the world's most stupendous slumber party?

A Sampling of Tweets about the Treehouse Ten

Zepp Janzaruk @srsly_zepp
Wow. U guys R awesome. Never come out!!!!!!!! #treehouse10

← ⟲ 146 ♡ 380

Ana-Karina Agriesti @AnaKarAg19
#treehouse10, we ROOT 4 CHANGE! Stay in there as long as you can!

← ⟲ 1.2K ♡ 5.6K

Charlie Horn @greathornspoon
#treehouse10 what a bunch of stupid kids. so glad they're not in our country anymore.

← ⟲ 201 ♡ 335

Adair Noll @AdairNoll
#treehouse10 need a good grounding. We're two EZ on kids 2day.

← ⟲ 21K ♡ 18.4K

Tweet & Potatoes @tweet_n_taters
I bet parents of #treehouse10 are glad theyre gone. #bunchofbrats!

← ⟲ 34 ♡ 251

Katya @ barakettKB

#treehouse10 can i join you? send me an
invite pleez?? will bring cupcakes!

  826 1.1K

Urmi K. @1andOnlyUrmi

I hope police & parents find a way to get
#treehouse10 kids down soon. They must
have a plan to force them out, right?

 677  400

"SUPER JOEY VS. THE PARENTS!!!"
(A COMIC ADVENTURE BY JOEY RAMUNDO)

How to Fill the Perfect Water Balloon

by Logan Litz

1. Buy it!

Real water balloons pop way better than regular party balloons, because they're thinner. In a pinch, you can use regular ones, but in my expert opinion, they're not as good.

2. Stretch it!

You have to stretch every balloon before you fill it with water. If you don't, you'll waste a whole bunch, because they'll pop when you fill them. Blow up each balloon with air, the same way you'd blow up a regular balloon. Try to make a good farting noise with the balloon while you let the air out. (You don't have to do that last part, but it makes the stretching step more fun.)

3. Tug it!

Next you have to stretch the neck of the balloon so it won't tear when you put it around the faucet. Stick two fingers inside the opening of the balloon and tug a little. Super easy!

4. Fill it!

Carefully attach the neck of the balloon to a water faucet. It's smartest to use a faucet over a sink, because if the balloon pops, all the water just goes down the drain. (Don't bring a hose into the living room and try to fill the balloons over your mom's favorite rug, trust me.) Hold the balloon at the bottom, and turn the water on LOW. Turn off the faucet before the water is all the way up to the neck. You'll need a little bit of air space to tie the balloon.

5. Tie it!

Keep one hand on the bottom of the balloon, and pinch the neck with your other hand while you wiggle the balloon off the faucet. Tug on the neck a few times, and then loop it around the first two fingers of your pinching hand. Pull the end through the loop to tie a knot.

6. Smash it!

Store up as many water balloons as you can, and then throw them at whoever you want!

Slumber-Party Fatigue
8+ days after what happened happened

As one week in the treehouse turned into two, one thing became very clear—none of the parents planned on giving in to the kids' demands any time soon.

At first, the Treehouse Ten were confused. After all, how hard would it have been for Tabitha's grandma to give her a lizard? Or for Jolee's parents to play a round of Scrabble with her? Didn't their parents *want* them to come home?

But the more they learned about the situation down on the ground (crowding around Uncle Huck's phone during his frequent visits), the better they began to understand. This wasn't just about them anymore. And it wasn't just about their parents, either.

"Sure, Maurizio Squizzato could agree not to ground his daughter over her excessive reading habits," one journalist wrote. *"But what's stopping her from climbing back into that treehouse one week later, when she decides what she really wants is a trip to space camp or a pony?"* ("I don't even *like* ponies!" Squizzy exclaimed when she

read that.) *"It's the principle of the thing, of course. If these parents don't stand up to their children now, adults everywhere will be fighting this same battle for centuries to come."*

So the parents weren't giving in. Instead, they seemed to be focusing on making the kids return to U.S. soil all on their own. Every night, as soon as the sun set, the policemen on the ground below shined fiery yellow spotlights straight through the treehouse windows, blinding everyone inside with burning-bright light. Towering speakers were set up on Winnie's parents' lawns, too, to blast out ear-shattering music.

"Tell me why!" the speakers blared, from sundown to sunup, the same hideous song, over and over in an endless, nightmarish loop. *"Ain't nothing but a heartache!"*

Night after night, the treehouse was unbearably bright and overwhelmingly loud. No one could sleep. And no one was happy.

"Sleep deprivation," Uncle Huck explained, during one of his visits. "They think if they keep you all from sleeping, you'll be so miserable you'll *beg* to leave."

"They can torture us all they want," Lyle grumbled, his eyes red and bleary. (When Lyle was tired, he got very grumbly.) "We're not coming down till they give in to our demands."

"Yeah!" Squizzy shouted out the open window to the crowd below. (When Squizzy was tired, she got very shouty.) "You hear that? Bring on your worst!"

So the kids didn't get much sleep. But they weren't giving in, either. Just like the parents, they had lots of people cheering them on. Every day, a new stack of boxes appeared on the mailbox platform, filled with supplies. Water bottles and chocolate syrup, grape soda and instant oatmeal. A hot plate for cooking. A fire extinguisher, in case the hot plate set the treehouse ablaze. Packs of T-shirts and fresh underwear and socks. Earplugs and sleep masks. Hand sanitizer and deodorant. Even a hot dog hat and a Hello Kitty poster. (Those last two things weren't especially useful.)

During the day, the Treehouse Ten did their best to catch up on sleep. And when they weren't dealing with mini disasters (like the time Joey clogged the toilet, and it took nearly two hours to fix it because no one knew how to use a plunger), they tried to do all the stupendous slumber party things they'd so enjoyed when they first climbed up the rope ladder.

They played games.

They sang songs.

They told stories.

Aayush experimented with the different foods they'd been sent, creating all sorts of interesting recipes on their new hot plate. On Sunday, he invented his best one yet, for marshmallow Cheetos treats. (Joey argued they were a waste of perfectly good Cheetos, but Aayush ignored him.)

VERY glad we never needed to use that!
— Squizzy

✓
I can't believe you put this part in here, Winnie! I'm sorry, okay? Sheesh!
— Joey

✓
That was definitely a gross day.
— Squizzy

Aayush's Extra-Gooey Marshmallow Cheetos Treats

NOTE:

Unless you live in a treehouse with only other kids around, you should have a grown-up help you make these, because the marshmallows get super hot on the stove and the Cheetos can be hard to stir. Plus, then you can make the grown-up wash the pot after, which is the worst part.

OTHER NOTE:

Winnie, this recipe is also really good with Froot Loops instead of Cheetos!

INGREDIENTS:
- 3 tbsp butter (plus extra for greasing the pan)
- 10 oz. mini marshmallows
- 1 bag (8.5 oz) crunchy Cheetos

EQUIPMENT:
- 9x9 baking dish
- very large pot
- spatula
- butter knife

1. Grease the bottoms and sides of the baking dish. Set it aside.

2. In the pot, melt the butter over medium-low heat, stirring often. When the butter is completely melted, add the marshmallows and stir constantly, until everything is totally melted and smooth (about 3 minutes).

3. Very quickly, add the Cheetos to the pot. Mix them in until they're evenly coated with marshmallow goo. Turn off the heat.

4. Transfer the Cheetos mixture to the baking dish and smoosh it down evenly with a spatula. Let cool, at least 15 minutes, then cut into squares and eat!

Logan and Brogan climbed out the windows whenever they got a chance. They swung from the branches and shimmied up to the roof, teasing the grown-ups below by pretending they were going to escape on the zip line. (Tabitha warned them they'd break an arm or something, but the twins didn't listen.)

For days, Squizzy read and read every book she could get her hands on—although by Monday, somehow even books didn't seem interesting to her anymore. (Uncle Huck brought her new books from the library, but she didn't crack open a single one of them.)

Joey, as it turned out, had become a minor internet celebrity, thanks to the *Super Joey* comic he'd mailed to his hero, local comic book artist Nolan Blight, who'd posted copies of Joey's work online. Joey spent his time churning out new adventures as fast as he could. (Squizzy, once she was sick of her own books, made lots of suggestions for new plotlines, but Joey didn't like any of them.)

On Tuesday, Greta ran out of embroidery thread for her friendship bracelets and got in a tug-of-war with Lyle over the last roll of dental floss. Jolee invented a new form of Scrabble, called Elbbarcs, which was exactly the same as regular Scrabble, except that you had to spell everything backward. (No one would play either game with her. Everyone was pretty tired of

yeah, i sort of wish we'd paid more attention to tabitha.
—logan

You're telling me!
—Brogan

✓ Winnie, you didn't say that Nolan Blight created <u>Blight Boy and Wrench Monkey!</u> (I still can't even believe he READ my comic! He's so cool!)
—Joey

∥ Your comic would be so much better if you'd just listen to me, Joey! —Squizzy

∥ No way I'm ever giving Super Joey a "red-headed orphan romantic interest," Squizz.
—Joey

✗ Dental floss is for oral hygiene, Greta, not art projects!!
—Lyle

Scrabble.) And Tabitha made a surprisingly cool stuffed lizard out of the green toe socks they'd received the week before. (Buttons liked the lizard as much as Tabitha did, which led to the second tug-of-war of the day.)

If you want to make a red ackie, use a red sock with yellow dots!
—Tabitha

How to Make a Stuffed Lizard Out of Toe Socks

by Tabitha Borchers

Materials

- one toe sock
- scissors
- safety pins
- scrap of white felt (optional)
- needle and thread
- black marker or black embroidery thread
- stuffing (scraps of old T-shirts or uncooked rice work great, too!)

Instructions

1. Cut off the toes of the sock, in one straight line.

2. Snip apart each individual toe, and set them aside to use later.

3. Fold the sock into thirds, and stick safety pins in the corners of each of the folds so you know where the thirds are when you unfold the sock.

4. Unfold the sock. The bottom third (where the toes used to be) will be the lizard's face, the middle will be its body, and the top third will be its tail.

5. If you're using white felt for eyes, cut out two big circles. (You can trace a quarter if you want the circles to be even.)

Attach the circles to the face part of the sock with safety pins, then sew them on with your needle and thread. Using your marker or black embroidery thread and a needle, add pupils to the lizard's eyes.

6. If you don't have any felt, you can just draw eyes directly on the sock.

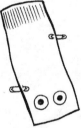

7. Grab the four smallest toe parts, and fill them with a tiny bit of stuffing. These will be the lizard's feet. Attach the stuffed feet to the middle part of the lizard's body with safety pins, then sew each foot in place with your needle and thread.

8. Use a safety pin to mark a spot in the exact middle of the topmost part of the sock. Then, with your scissors, make a cut from the safety pin just above the lizard's back right foot to the top safety pin. Make the same cut on the other side. You have now formed the shape of the lizard's tail.

9. Remove all of the safety pins, and turn the lizard inside out. Use your needle and thread to sew shut the tail on both sides. Turn the lizard right side out again.

10. Fill the lizard with stuffing. Make him as smooshy or as flat as you want! Then take the last toe part and place it between the lizard's two lips, so that about ¼ inch is stuck inside. This will be the lizard's tongue. Secure the tongue and the two lips together with a safety pin.

11. Use your needle and thread to sew shut the lizard's lips. Now you have your very own stuffed lizard!

As for Winnie, she did her best to finish up her local history report, with the help of Uncle Huck's laptop for research. But just as the deadline drew uncomfortably close, the grown-ups on the ground below shut down all internet access to the treehouse, in yet another attempt to force out the kids. Winnie had absolutely no idea how she was going to finish her report and pass fifth grade now. Her friends tried to help, but it wasn't like they could dig up much useful information for a local history report about a tree, even if the tree was the very one they were currently living in. (To tell the truth, though, Winnie's friends were being a little too shouty or grumbly, or too focused on whatever *they* were doing to be very helpful anyway.)

Things were looking bleak.

On Wednesday afternoon, twelve full days after she'd first climbed into her treehouse and refused to come down, Winnie turned her Artist Vision on her friends again, observing them in the shifted light.

Their bleary eyes.

Their mumble-hissing arguments about everything from dirty dishes to Go Fish.

The way everyone's games and songs and stories were seeming just a little less fun, a little more tiring.

The slumber party, Winnie observed, was getting old. But unlike at a real sleepover, no one could simply go home when they felt like leaving. There were too many people watching, wondering, *waiting* for the Treehouse Ten's next move.

So the war raged on. And all over the world, kids and grown-ups held their breath, hardly daring to guess who would break first.

As it turned out, it wasn't a *who* that broke.

It was a *what*.

The DOs and DON'Ts of Climbing Winnie's Linden Tree

by Brogan Litz

Do! squiggle yourself out the window when you want some fresh air or just feel like throwing water balloons at some grown-ups.

Don't! forget to hold on tight.

Do! either squirm out onto the largest branch on your belly or grip it hard with your legs as you slide on your butt.

Don't! try to stand up without holding on to something!

Do! keep your body low—that's the best way to balance.

Don't! throw all your water balloons at once—you'll be sad you used them all up, and your brother will probably refuse to fill any more for you, so you'll have to go back inside the treehouse and do it yourself.

Do! climb up the rope ladder along the side of the treehouse to the roof. The roof is the best place to launch water balloons at grown-ups.

Don't! forget to bring your backpack outside with you, so you can pack all your water balloons in there.

Do! sit in the zip-line seat on top of the roof. It's a great view from up there, and it will really freak out everyone on the ground!

Don't! forget to stay alert when you're in the zip-line seat!!!!

Definitely Don't! accidentally push yourself forward on the zip line when you're reaching for a water balloon in your backpack!!!!!

Absolutely, Positively Don't! freak out when you start zooming down the zip line, and try to jump off onto the roof instead of holding on to the handlebars above you!!!!!!!!!!

Seriously, No Matter What You Do, Don't! fall off the treehouse roof!!

That was SO
SCARY, Brogan!!!!
—Jolee

You're telling me!!!!
—Brogan

Glenbrook Hospital
876 Lavender Road
Glenbrook, PA 19066

Patient Name: Brogan Litz
Service Date: Thursday, April 27

Charge Summary

Forearm X-Ray
Forearm Cast
Doctor Fee (Non-Surgical)
Pain Medication
Ambulance Service

The Worst Night

13 days after what happened happened

I t was *awful* when Brogan fell off the roof on Thursday morning. Inside, every one of the Treehouse Ten heard the sickening *thump!* Outside, parents and policemen and reporters shrieked in terror. When Winnie and her friends watched the news footage later, it was hard not to feel freaked out all over again—Brogan on the ground, with his arm snapped out beside him at an angle an arm should *never* be, howling in pain.

The worst part was the minute right after the fall, when no one was sure what to do. The police didn't think they could cross the barricade to reach Brogan, and the Treehouse Ten were paralyzed at the window, worrying about climbing down.

It was Logan who saved the day. He scrambled down the rope ladder like a monkey, and dragged his brother across the barricade to the cops. He tried to go with Brogan to the hospital, too, but Brogan pushed him back so he'd stay in the treehouse.

Logan didn't talk much after that, the whole rest of the

day. You could tell he was really worried about his brother. No one else really felt like talking either. It didn't seem like a good time to play games or sing songs or tell stories. Mostly everyone stayed pretty quiet, pretty serious, even as the afternoon wore on and the crowd outside began chanting for them to come down. *"For your own safety!"* the grown-ups shouted. (Squizzy went around slamming all the windows and snapping shut the curtains, but the Treehouse Ten could still hear them.) And as hard as she tried, Winnie couldn't focus on finishing her local history report, which she somehow needed to get to Mr. B by the next day to have any hope of passing the fifth grade.

Not long before the sun set that evening—minutes before the blazing yellow beam of the spotlight and the hideous music pierced the quiet—the mailbox light on the wall turned red. And when Lyle yanked up the mail platform, they discovered a single puffy white envelope. It was addressed to Logan, and inside was a note.

Logan—

I'm fine, just broke my dumb arm.
Mom and Dad are so mad, they won't
let me watch ANY TV, even though
what the heck else am I supposed to

i wasn't worried in a baby way. in, like, a brother way.
—logan

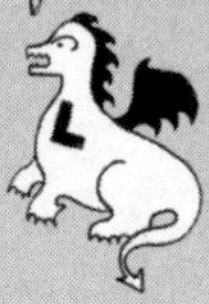

do now that my arm is broken????
I told them YOU won't come down till
they change their minds and let us
watch anything we want (even Dragon
Destroyers!!!!) You have to do
whatever you can so the kids win.

TREEHOUSE TEN FOREVER!

From,
Brogan

P.S. This might make it easier for
you all to stay up there—I found it
in Kyle's room, from his old phone.
Keep it secret that you have it,
though, OK? I know you can't get
online, but have Joey text Kyle if
you need anything.

Underneath the note was a charger for Joey's phone. (Joey cheered with joy when he saw it.)

"Brogan's right, you know," Squizzy said, reading the note over Logan's shoulder. Her voice was shoutier than normal, because of how tired she was. "About doing whatever we can to win the war."

I do not get shouty
when I'm tired!
— Squizzy

It's a memoir,
Squizzy. Winnie has
to write the truth.
— Lyle

"Sure," Lyle grumbled. He was grumblier than normal, because of how tired he was. "But what are we supposed to *do* exactly, besides stay up here? We're already doing everything we can."

Squizzy folded her arms over her chest, thinking. "Maybe we should make a new list of demands," she said. "A shorter one. With only one or two things on it, the things that are most important to everyone, like a total ban on grounding. The parents might actually agree to that, if we aren't asking for so much dumb stuff. Then not only would we get to leave the treehouse, but we'd be proving we can make important decisions. Be independent."

"That's a pretty good idea," Tabitha said, nodding slowly.

"Yeah," Joey said. "Independent. I like it."

"I like it, too," Greta agreed.

Lyle, however, did *not* like it.

"The stuff we asked for wasn't dumb!" he snapped. "We demanded things we *want*. Things we *need*! We can't just ask for new stuff now. *That's* what would make us look dumb. Everyone would think we were just a bunch of kids who couldn't make up our minds. No one will *ever* take us seriously if we do that!"

"That's a good point," Aayush said, scratching his ear.

"We do have to look serious," Logan agreed.

"Exactly," Jolee added.

From her seat at the kitchen table, with her unfinished history report spread out before her, Winnie watched with an uncomfortable churning in her stomach, as each of her friends turned to look at her.

"Winnie?" Squizzy said, her arms still folded across her chest. "What do *you* think?"

"Yeah," Lyle said, and he began to grind his teeth, ever so slightly. "Who do you agree with?"

Winnie glanced at Buttons, who was smartly staying out of things, curled up all alone on the loft steps. When she looked back at her friends, they were still staring at her, waiting for her answer.

So Winnie did the only thing she could think to do—she turned on her Artist Vision and observed each of her friends in the shifted light.

Squizzy's fingers, twitching as she tapped her elbow.

Tabitha's eyes, narrowed to slits.

Joey's grumpy head nods.

Greta's huffy breathing, *in-and-out, in-and-out*, waiting for Winnie's response.

Lyle's quiet teeth-grinding.

Aayush's *scratch-scratch-scratch*ing of his ear.

The blotchy red spots on Logan's cheeks.

Jolee's slow, frustrated blinking.

Each of Winnie's friends, she observed, was waiting for

her to pick a side, whether Winnie wanted to pick one or not.

Winnie took a deep breath. "I think," she said carefully, "that if I don't finish my local history report before tomorrow, I'm going to fail fifth grade. So maybe we don't have to argue about this right this second. Maybe we can figure things out in the morning."

Winnie didn't need to use her Artist Vision to observe that none of her friends liked that response at all.

Winnie didn't need to use her Artist Vision to observe that none of her friends had even *listened*.

"You have to take a side!" Squizzy said, extra shouty.

"You're the tiebreaker!" Lyle told her, extra grumbly. "Who do you agree with?"

Winnie did not want to take a side. She did not want to be a tiebreaker. Because the truth was, she thought that both of her friends were a little right.

Squizzy was right about fighting for independence. There was no point of any of them having gone up in the treehouse in the first place if they didn't get *something* out of it.

And Lyle was right about needing to be taken seriously. None of the parents would agree to give them *anything* if they acted like little kids.

But Winnie thought both her friends were a little wrong, too. Ignoring the other person and acting like theirs was the only solution—that was no way to get any of them anywhere.

Ha!!
—Squizzy

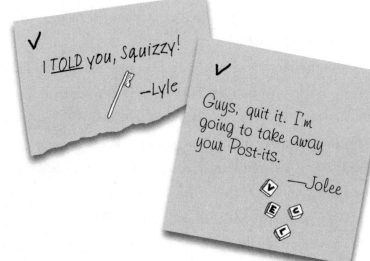

I *TOLD* you, Squizzy!

—Lyle

Guys, quit it. I'm going to take away your Post-its.

—Jolee

Watching Squizzy and Lyle glare at each other across the treehouse made Winnie's stomach churn inside her like a washing machine that had gone off balance. And Winnie knew from too much experience that when she got that off-balance churning in her stomach, she couldn't count on the two people who'd started it to make the churning stop.

She looked at Squizzy.

And she looked at Lyle.

And she looked down at her unfinished history report.

It was in that moment that the fiery yellow spotlight blazed through the treehouse window, and the insufferable grown-up music blasted all around them. And for the first time since the parents had begun their sleep deprivation tactics, Winnie was actually relieved. She couldn't have told her friends what she thought if she'd wanted to—there was no way for them to hear her.

But the Treehouse Ten (well, Nine now, without Brogan) didn't need to hear to fight. They divided themselves up without a single word—Squizzy, Tabitha, Greta, and Joey arranging their sleeping bags in the lounge area downstairs, and Lyle, Aayush, Logan, and Jolee crowded in the loft. As for Winnie, she joined Buttons on the stairs, right smack in the middle of all her friends, scrunched into an uncomfortable knot all night, with the yellow spotlight burning patches into her vision and the screeching music eating away at her brain.

Just past two in the morning, with no one even close to sleep, Squizzy tacked a sheet of paper to the trunk in the middle of the treehouse, where everyone would see it. As Winnie squinted to make out the words, the churning in her stomach grew worse than ever.

NEW TREEHOUSE TIMETABLE

(AKA how to split up our time in the treehouse so our SMART side doesn't have to be around Lyle's STUPID side)

(P.S. Winnie, everything would be a lot better for everyone if you just said who you agreed with!)

DS4 = Downstairs Four (Squizzy, Greta, Tabitha & Joey)
US4 = Upstairs Four (Lyle, Aayush, Logan & Jolee)
W = Winnie

	6:00am – 8:59am	9:00am – 11:59am	12:00pm – 2:59pm
bathroom	DS4	W	US4
kitchen	US4	DS4	W
art area/ mailbox	W	US4	DS4

This was so messed up, Squizzy. I can't believe you tried to tell us when we could pee.

—Joey

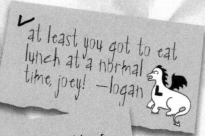

at least you got to eat lunch at a normal time, joey! —logan

All right, maybe things did get a little out of hand for a while.

—Squizzy

3:00pm–5:59pm	6:00pm–8:59pm	9:00pm–11:59pm	12:00am–2:29am	3:00am–5:59am
DS4	W	US4	DS4	W
US4	DS4	W	US4	DS4
W	US4	DS4	W	US4

The Great Escape
14 days after what happened happened

In her entire life, Winnie had never felt so rotten.

All night, Winnie sat crouched on the loft steps next to Buttons. Half of her friends glared angrily up at her from the first floor, and the other half glared angrily down at her from the second. The five pages of her not-quite-finished local history report, which Buttons had wedged himself on top of, seemed to be glaring at her, too. Winnie's stomach churned and churned inside her, until she felt like it might just burst. ◉

By the time the sun began to poke its way back into the sky Friday morning, Winnie knew she couldn't sit there churning any longer. So, when the spotlights snapped off outside, and the blazing yellow glow inside the treehouse dimmed, Winnie pressed the balls of her feet gently against the loft steps, getting ready.

When the music stopped blasting, and the only sounds that worked their way through the windows were the birds' chirpings, Winnie carefully shifted Buttons off her report.

I'm really sorry we made you feel so bad, Winnie. ☹ —Jolee

Yeah, but I guess if this didn't happen then nothing that happened later would have happened either, right? So it's sort of a good thing? —Aayush

Aayush is right. Glad we made you feel so awful, Winnie! (That was a joke, btw.) —Lyle

I bet Winnie could've figured out that was a joke, Lyle. She's not a moron. —Squizzy

Squizz, will you stop using up all the Post-its for no reason?? —Lyle

YOU stop using all the Post-its, Lyle!!!!!!! —Squizzy

OK, guys, this is getting crazy again. —Jolee

When she heard the deep *in-and-out*s, *in-and-out*s of her friends drifting off groggily in their sleeping bags, Winnie slowly rose to her feet.

When the handful of night-patrolling grown-ups on the ground below headed to their cars to swap with the morning shift, Winnie tiptoed down to the art station, her not-quite-finished local history report wedged deep in her armpit. She opened a cubby door and removed a single item: her new zip-line helmet from Uncle Huck. Then, with her friends still snoozing and the adults on the ground focused elsewhere, Winnie quietly, quietly crept to the window. She quietly, quietly lifted the glass.

Winnie darted one last glance at Buttons, to make sure he was okay with her decision. And because he was the world's greatest cat, he offered her the tiniest of nods.

Winnie took a deep breath and strapped her helmet to her head. She tucked the twelve carefully handwritten pages of her not-quite-finished local history report in the back band of her blue polka-dot pajamas. She climbed out onto the widest branch of the linden tree, grabbed the rope ladder attached to the side of the treehouse, and made her way to the roof. She plopped herself down in the zip-line seat, grabbing on tight to the handlebars with both hands. And she kicked off with both feet.

As Winnie zipped through the crisp April air—down

through the branches, across her parents' lawns, across the street, past the cars of the unsuspecting adults below—her stomach stopped its churning. It was all over, she told herself. She'd made the right decision in escaping. Everything would work out just fine. It would.

But just before she landed on the roof of Uncle Huck's house, the twelve carefully handwritten pages of Winnie's not-quite-finished local history report dislodged themselves from the back band of her blue polka-dot pajamas. And all Winnie could do was watch as her weeks of hard work scattered in the wind, rushing off in all directions.

Part III

How It All Ended

Advice and Toaster Waffles
14 days after what happened happened

Later, Uncle Huck would tell Winnie that he was pretty ter-rified to be jolted out of bed by his pajama-wearing niece stomping down on the skylight right above his bed. But as soon as she was safely inside the house, he seemed very happy to have her there.

Winnie, on the other hand, was *not* so happy. "My *report*!" she wailed, whipping her helmet off her head. "It's due today! There's no *way* I can redo everything now!"

"Winnie," Uncle Huck said, taking hold of both her shoulders to try to calm her. "We'll figure it out. I promise."

"But I'm going to *fail* fifth *grade*!"

Winnie thought Uncle Huck would say some reassuring grown-up thing then, like, "Take a deep breath," or "Count to ten, okay?" But what he said instead was, "Breakfast."

"Breakfast?"

"That's the only thing we need to worry about right this second, got it?"

Winnie wiped a sniffle from her nose and nodded. Breakfast was something she could worry about.

When they reached the kitchen, Uncle Huck got to work shifting messy stacks of papers to make room for Winnie to sit. Winnie was used to this when she visited. Maybe it was Uncle Huck's "artistic mind," or maybe her mom was right that he was just a slob. Whatever the reason, Winnie's uncle was always leaving printouts and newspapers and drafting plans for new projects wherever they happened to land. And where they landed was *everywhere*.

"Sit, sit, sit," Uncle Huck told Winnie, moving a heap of papers into the sink. "What's going on? Are you okay? Tell me why you're here."

Winnie sat. And she tried to think of the best way to explain things. "My report," she said. "I needed to finish it. I thought if I came here I could . . ." But then she trailed off, realizing that perhaps her local history report wasn't the *only* reason she'd fled the treehouse.

"My friends are fighting," she finished at last. She looked down at her hands. "I was in the middle. I didn't like it."

Uncle Huck opened a cupboard above the sink. It was completely empty. "So what are you going to do about it?" he asked, tugging open the dishwasher and pulling a glass from the top rack. After a quick swipe with a dishtowel, he set the glass in front of Winnie.

Winnie shrugged. "I *tried* to talk to them," she said. "Just like I tried to talk to Mom and Dad. But it didn't work. They didn't listen. No one ever listens to me. I'm not very good at talking, I guess."

"Oh, I don't think that's true," Uncle Huck replied, grabbing a carton of orange juice from the refrigerator. He opened it, sniffed it, and then set it beside the glass. "You talk to me just fine. You ask me, the problem's on their end. All of them."

Winnie slowly poured herself some juice. "It's still a problem, though, isn't it?" she said.

"I suppose so," Uncle Huck admitted. He frowned and made his way to the freezer. "So maybe you can't make your friends hear what you need them to," he told Winnie. "Maybe no one can. Toaster waffle?"

"Sure." Winnie eyed her juice. It was the kind with the pulp. Winnie hated pulp. She pushed the glass away. "So what am I supposed to do?" she asked, as Uncle Huck toasted their breakfast. "If I can't make them hear?"

Uncle Huck was silent until two waffles popped from the toaster, crisp and golden. "Maybe you need to change your tactics," he told Winnie, placing a waffle in front of her on a paper towel.

"I don't have any tactics," Winnie replied. She gave her

waffle a nibble. When she noticed Uncle Huck raising his eyebrows at her, she told him, "I'm not *good* at anything." He raised them higher. "Nothing useful, anyway. I'm good at art." He nodded. "Doodling. Painting." She thought a little more. "Artist Vision."

"Aha!" Uncle Huck slapped his hand on the table so hard that Winnie's glass jumped, sloshing pulpy orange juice onto an old newspaper. "And you said you had no useful skills."

Winnie scooped up the newspaper to try to mop up some of the juice. "You think I can solve all my problems with *Artist Vision*?"

"Well, no," Uncle Huck said. "Obviously not. Failing fifth grade, for example, that's probably a whole different kettle of fish. As for your friends, though . . ." He took a swig of orange juice, straight from the container. "I wouldn't be surprised if your Artist Vision helped you with that quite a bit."

Winnie's eye landed on a particularly curious advertisement for a museum exhibit about medical oddities in the juice-stained paper she was holding. "Maybe . . . ," she said slowly, mulling things over.

"In any case," Uncle Huck told her, "you should probably move quickly." He scooped a different newspaper out of the teetering tower on the table, flipping through the articles about local artists and upcoming events, until he found the one he wanted. "Here." He jabbed his finger at a headline.

@

Once again a little
spilled orange juice
changes <u>everything!</u>

—Squizzy

"EMBASSY HISTORIAN" HIRED TO DISCOVER LOOPHOLE FOR RETRIEVING CHILDREN FROM TREEHOUSE

Winnie drank in the words slowly. If she didn't find a way to solve her problems before she was "retrieved" from her treehouse, everything would go back to the way it was before—or worse. And she definitely didn't want that.

"You really think I can fix things?" she asked Uncle Huck.

"No doubt in my mind," he said. "Although you're not solving anything here, eating waffles."

At that, Winnie had to laugh. Uncle Huck was right, as always.

Winnie scarfed down the rest of her waffle in two bites. Then, with her worries about breakfast completely resolved, she returned her helmet to her head.

"I'm going back," she told her uncle. "And I'm going to fix everything."

Uncle Huck smiled. "Excellent," he said. "Oh, and Winnie?"

She tightened the straps of her helmet. "Yeah?"

"Sometimes it helps to turn your Artist Vision on yourself, too, you know."

But Winnie was hardly listening. She was already busy formulating a plan.

When Winnie kicked off in the zip line five minutes later, zooming her way back to the very spot she'd only just escaped from, she was gripping several pages of newspaper under her arm.

TRANSCRIPT

The following is what was said on the Channel 10 Action News special report that aired the morning of Friday, April 28th—the same day Winnie escaped from (and returned to) her treehouse.

Amanda Howard, Channel 10 Action News Correspondent: This is Amanda Howard, with absolutely nothing to report. I hope something happens soon, because Frankie and I have been here for two weeks now, and we're getting a little sick of each other, ha-ha.

[The camera pans past Amanda's shoulder and up into the tree cover, where Winnie can be seen, a blue blur zipping toward the treehouse roof.]

Amanda Howard: Frankie, what are you doing? I know you're tired, but jeez. I'm over *here*.

Frank Quijata, Channel 10 Action News Cameraman: [voice heard off camera] *Um, Amanda? Turn around, okay?*

Amanda Howard: I think we better head back to you guys in the studio, Tom. Frankie here's getting a little loopy.

Frank Quijata: [voice heard off camera] *It's her, Amanda! It's the girl, Winnie! She's zip-lining toward the treehouse!*

Amanda Howard: How could the girl be heading toward the treehouse if she's already *in*— [Amanda finally spots Winnie; puts on her best professional voice] Tom, I see we have a bit of a scoop here. I, Amanda Howard, from Channel 10 Action News, can officially report that the leader of the Treehouse Ten, Gwinnie Majazz-Melody, is . . . [Camera focuses on the treehouse roof, where Winnie lands and quickly scrambles down through the window] . . . inside her treehouse.

[Amanda is silent for a moment, as the camera remains steady on the treehouse window. All that can be seen is a curtain rustling in the wind.]

Amanda Howard: [clears throat] Well, you heard it here first, folks. Everything's exactly the same as it was before. Stay tuned for more exciting updates on this breaking story. Back to you in the studio, Tom!

Winnie's Return

14+ days after what happened happened

When Winnie snuck her way back inside the treehouse, with her friends still snoozing in their sleeping bags, everything was exactly the way it was before she left. But somehow, everything was different, too.

That whole Friday and the day after, as Winnie's friends took turns using the kitchen and the art station and the bathroom, according to Squizzy's strict schedule, the mood in the treehouse was tense. No one talked much at all. Everyone seemed awfully grumpy. The whole time, Winnie kept to herself, sitting on the loft steps with Buttons curled on her lap. She was pushing thoughts about her not-turned-in local history report to the farthest corner of her mind. (Would she fail fifth grade now? Would all her friends go to middle school without her?) Instead of worrying about that, she observed her friends with her Artist Vision. She squinted her eyes and noted how the shifted light slanted off them.

I hated that schedule, Squizzy!

—Joey

Yeah, that was no fun at all.
—Tabitha

I'm sorry, guys, sheesh!
—Squizzy

She observed.

She noted.

And she doodled in her sketchbook.

And with each doodle she drew, Winnie's vision grew stronger. Sharper.

Her friends, Winnie realized as she watched and doodled, had come to the treehouse with very clear demands about what they wanted. But in the shifted light, Winnie began to see that perhaps what they *really* wanted was something else entirely.

Doodles in the Treehouse

(As Drawn by Winnie)

Aayush

Notes:
- spends kitchen time working on food experiments but never eats them
- spends rest of time writing notes, but throws them away (who is he writing to???)
- <u>makes Cheetos treats in shape of elephants</u>

Observations:
- feels bad about sister's stuffed elephant?

Logan

Notes:
- has lots of water balloons left but won't throw any of them
- always texting Brogan on Joey's phone
- cheeks are blotchy <u>(from crying?)</u>

Observations:
- misses Brogan? ✓

i was not crying! i was
allergic to the
treehouse. i think.
　　　　　　—logan

✓
Aw, that's so sweet,
Logan. You missed
me!!
　　　—Brogan

✓
shut up, brogan!
　　　—logan

Greta

Notes:

- wants to help Joey with comic book even when he ignores her ideas
- talks to Upstairs 4 even when Squizzy gets mad at her for it
- makes <u>friendship bracelets</u> for everybody, even though they already have tons

Observations:

- needs a best friend?

Tabitha

Notes:

- made 16 toe sock lizards in 2 days
- wakes up Buttons from naps for tug-of-wars
- <u>really excited when Jolee talked to her</u> (and Jolee was only complaining about her annoying sister again!)

Observations:

- lonely?

Joey

Notes:
- hardly uses phone anymore
- very grumpy when not his <u>time at art station</u>
- sending lots of new comic books out in mailbox

Observations:
- found a new hobby?

Jolee

Notes:
- playing lots of Scrabble solitaire
- keeps complaining about annoying sister (even though no one's asking!)
- checks mailbox 1,000 times a day for new mail

Observations:
- wants attention?

Squizzy

Notes:
- hasn't opened a book in 6 days (!!!!!)
- working on new demands so we can all <u>"decide about our own lives"</u>
- very shouty whenever someone (Lyle) disagrees with her!

Observations:
- wants more ~~indipen~~ independence?

Lyle

Notes:
- doesn't notice tooth collection is dusty (!!!)
- grinding his teeth without realizing (!!!!!!)
- grumbles about how he's <u>not just a dumb kid</u> who wants dumb stuff

Observations:
- wants to be taken seriously?

An Artist with a Plan

16+ days after what happened happened

That Sunday morning, more than two weeks after she'd first stormed into her treehouse and refused to come down, Winnie was done with doodling. And she knew that Uncle Huck had been right. Maybe she couldn't get her friends to listen to her, but maybe—with the help of a useful skill she'd had tucked up her sleeve all along—she could fix some of her problems anyway.

As soon as the clock read six a.m., Winnie used her scheduled art-station time to draft a letter. When she was done writing, she sealed the letter tight and addressed it and plopped it on the mailbox platform.

Then she wrote another.

And another.

By the time Squizzy informed Winnie at precisely nine a.m. that she needed to "move your butt out of the way for some *other* people—can't you read the timetable?" Winnie had

OK, so maybe I was being a <u>little</u> terrible right then. (Sorry, Winnie. ☹) —Squizzy

Joey, can I borrow your phone to take a photo?
—Lyle

dropped no fewer than eight letters, each tucked into a crisp envelope and carefully addressed, onto the mailbox platform.

Early that afternoon, the responses began to roll in. The first was a letter, addressed to Aayush in his little sister's blocky handwriting.

Dear Aayush,

I miss you. Come home ok?
Mom and Dad said if you come
home today they'll take us to the
mall so we can pick out a new elefant
together. They said it wasn't there
idea but it's a good idea anyway I
think. I will name the elefant Aayush
(after you).
Love,
Your sister Ash

After reading the letter, Aayush quickly packed up all his marshmallow elephant treats and his sleeping bag, too. "I . . . ," he told the group as he stood just beside the trapdoor, "I think I need to go. I . . ."

Squizzy was glaring at him, hands across her chest. Lyle was, too.

"But you can't leave!" Squizzy said, extra shouty. "We're fighting for *independence* here!"

"If you go now," Lyle told him, extra grumbly, "without getting what you demanded, then why should anyone ever take the rest of us seriously?"

Aayush frowned at both of them. He seemed unsure about what to say. But Winnie observed, from the way he clutched his sister's letter, that he knew what he wanted to do.

"We can't force Aayush to stay if he doesn't want to," Winnie told her friends. And when Aayush darted his eyes her way, she could tell she'd said something good. It calmed the washing-machine churning in her stomach, just a little, to know that she was helping. "He wants to go." She slowly spun the combination lock for him and pulled back the trapdoor. Winnie could see the patch of dirt that circled the linden tree, fifteen feet straight below her, and the rope ladder swaying slightly in the breeze. But she wasn't the one leaving. Not just yet.

"Tell your sister hi for me, okay?" Winnie told Aayush. And Aayush gave Winnie a quick hug before he scrambled down the ladder.

Everyone seemed pretty peeved that Aayush had left, including Logan . . . that is, until an hour later, when Logan's brother Kyle sent him a series of texts on Joey's phone.

yo Joey this is Kyle, give Logan the phone OK?

Hey Kyle it's Logan whats up?

DUDE, LOGAN, STOP BEING AN IDIOT AND COME HOME ALREADY!!

?????

I know B said to stay in that stupid treehouse forever but he totally misses you OK?

B won't even let anyone sign his cast till you sign it first

Did Mom and Dad say it was OK to watch our show yet?

No

Dude, they're never gonna give in about that

They're really pissed

So I should stay up here then

YOU SHOULD STOP BEING AN IDIOT.

(I say that as your loving older brother)

Seriously tho. Brogan's really bummed without you

I've never seen him so sad

You have to come home OK?

Who cares about your stupid show?

But B told me to stay up here until mom and dad give in

BROGAN IS AN IDIOT TOO YOU MORON!!!

That's why you have to come back. So you can be morons together

OK????

Everyone was pretty peeved when Logan decided to leave, too—everyone but Winnie. "Sorry," Logan told the group, his

backpack slung over his shoulder. "I know you're mad, but"—
he glanced at the texts one more time before handing Joey back
his phone—"I have to go." He wiped away a sniffle. "It's important. Brogan's more important than a TV show."

Even after she closed the trapdoor behind him, Winnie
could hear the cheers of Logan's parents outside, as they hugged
their son tight. And the noise calmed the washing-machine
churning in her stomach, just the tiniest bit more.

On Monday morning, a pamphlet arrived for Greta.

On Tuesday afternoon, there was a letter for Joey.

And . . .

And . . .

As more and more *somethings* began to appear in the mailbox, the Treehouse Ten quickly dwindled to a Treehouse One.

Which, as it turned out, had been Winnie's plan all along.

CRAFT CAMP!

Young artists and makers,
come join us in May for
A FULL WEEK of arty fun!

Are you between the ages of
9 and 12? Do you like all things
CRAFTY? Then our after-school
CRAFT CAMP is for you!

CRAFT BINGE!
For 5 days, you will make friends,
memories, and best of all
LOTS OF COOL CRAFTS!

Jewelry!
Felt Making!
Needlework!
Pottery!
Papier-Mâché!
Glass Etching
Stuffed Anima
Beadwork!
Wood Carvir

Greta,

We just learned about this camp and thought you'd enjoy it. Know anyone up in that treehouse who might want to come with you? (Someone who's pretty great at making stuffed lizards, maybe?) Sounds like the perfect place to find a best friend.

We love you and miss you!

Love,
Mom and Dad

P.S. The camp starts this afternoon, just so you know!
P.P.S. Tell Tabitha her grandma thinks Craft Camp sounds great, too!

Nolan Blight

9 S. South St. / Philadelphia, PA 19103
blightoftheworld@blightdraws.com

Tuesday, May 2nd

Mr. Joseph Ramundo
The Treehouse Where All the Kids Are Holed Up
Glenbrook, PA 19066

Dear Joey:

I wanted to officially thank you for sending me your *Super Joey* comics. As I hope you've figured out by now, I'm a *huge* fan. Ⓖ

It's been suggested to me that you might like to stop by my studio and see how real comics are made, and I think it's a great idea. So, no rush or anything (since I bet you're having a pretty stellar time up in that treehouse), but when you *do* decide to come back to Earth, you and your parents are invited for a tour of my studio. I'll even give you a sneak peek at my latest issue of *Blight Boy and Wrench Monkey*, before it's released to the public. ✓

                        Your pal,

                        Nolan

Joey screamed when he read this part of the letter.

—Squizzy

Joey screamed again here. Just so everyone knows.

—Squizzy

**The Glenbrook Community
Center presents**

THE FIRST ANNUAL
JUNIOR SEMIREGIONAL

TOURNAMENT

Saturday, May 6th
10AM to 2PM
Open to children ages 6–18
All skill levels welcome

Jolee–

We thought you might want to go to this. Could be fun! We'll get a babysitter for Ainslee and cheer you on louder than anyone.

Love, Mom and Dad

Dear Sonia,

You've been up in that treehouse an awful long time, and I got to thinking. Okay, so maybe your mom and I can't give you everything you ask for (and, to be honest, we do need to have a conversation about your reading habits), but you're getting older every day and more mature, and we know you need your independence. So when you're ready, we're here to talk. What do you want, honey? Higher allowance? Later bedtime? You come down, we'll discuss.

Love,
Dad

SPECIAL EXHIBIT

The World's Largest Human Tooth

(fifteen times the size of a standard molar!)

Lyle, we know we don't always take your tooth collecting very seriously, but we thought you'd want to go to this. Ends soon!

Love,

Mom Dana & Mom Kate

Limited Engagement

Showing through Sunday, May 7th

MÜTTER MUSEUM

"Treehouse 10" End Two-Week Siege⊚

Wednesday, May 3rd
BY MARGARET WEINSNOGGLE

GLENBROOK—Parents around the world breathed sighs of relief this morning, as the second to last of the so-called Treehouse 10—all fifth-graders from local Tulip Street Elementary School—ended their 19-day standoff. Cheers could be heard from blocks away when the ninth child climbed down from the treehouse between the properties of Dr. Alexis Maraj and Dr. Varun Malladi, running to hug his tearful parents. Everyone seemed relieved that the disagreement had at last come to a peaceful end.

Only one member of the Treehouse Ten still refuses to return to American soil. As of press time, Winifred Malladi-Maraj, the treehouse's original resident, remains inside, with no sign of when she might leave. Neither of Winifred's parents chose to comment.

⊚
Winnie, you already put this article in the memoir. At the very beginning, remember?
—Brogan

⊚
Duh, Brogan, she did it on purpose (right, Winnie?). It's called "bookending" or whatever. Mr. B totally talked about it in our lit unit.
—Squizzy

Another Regular Wednesday
19 days after what happened happened

"**D**o you think I'm dumb for leaving?" Lyle asked Winnie on Wednesday morning, as he gazed down at the patch of dirt circling the linden tree fifteen feet below. His feet were dangling from the open trapdoor, and his backpack (with his tooth display case tucked inside) was strapped tightly to his shoulders.

He was the last of Winnie's friends to leave the treehouse.

"Why would I think you were dumb?" Winnie asked him.

"Because I kept *saying* I wouldn't leave until I got what I demanded. And I didn't get what I demanded. None of us did."

What Winnie observed, with her Artist Vision, was that her friend's shoulders were more relaxed than they'd been in days. His teeth were no longer grinding.

He was making the right decision.

"What would be *dumb*," Winnie told him, "is to stay in a treehouse forever, just so you didn't look dumb."

At that, Lyle laughed. He turned his attention back to the ground. Grown-ups outside were hollering at his feet, pleading with him to come down, but Winnie knew that Lyle would only leave when he was good and ready.

"You'll be okay up here by yourself?" he asked Winnie.

"Sure," she said. Already the washing-machine churning was barely a *swish*. "I like it here. And anyway, I've got Buttons."

Lyle could hardly argue with that.

When Winnie had spun the lock shut behind the last of her friends, she let out a deep sigh of relief. She hadn't solved all the problems of the world, not by a long shot. (There was still the matter of failing fifth grade to deal with, and—she glanced out the windows, beyond the patch of dirt that circled the linden tree—well, other things, too.) But for the moment, things were good enough.

Winnie picked her way through the mess her friends had left behind—forgotten sleeping bags, an abandoned draft of *Super Joey*, granola bar wrappers and wadded-up napkins and a smooshed marshmallow Cheetos elephant. Outside, the reporters and parents and police had already packed up, leaving traces of their own—ruts in the grass and bits of litter. For the first time in what felt like ages, there was only quiet drifting in from the window. When she reached the trunk in the center of the treehouse, Winnie tugged down Squizzy's timeline and crumpled it up and threw it on the floor. Then she poured herself a bowl of Froot Loops and settled at the kitchen table. Buttons leapt into her lap, snuggling into a comfy position.

"Guess it's just you and me now, huh?" Winnie said as she scratched under his chin. "Just another regular Wednesday." In response, Buttons purred his happiest purr.

Winnie slurped up her Froot Loops, happy to have things back to exactly the way they'd started. Except . . .

She glanced out the north-facing window for any sign of movement from her mom's house.

She squinted out the south-facing window, at her dad's house.

Nope . . . exactly the way they'd started.

When the sky outside grew dark and the air grew still, Winnie and Buttons tucked themselves under their soft, ratty quilt and gazed out the skylight above them, watching the leaves and the stars and the world. But Winnie couldn't sleep. Not a wink. Because now that she was all alone in the treehouse, there was no one left to turn her Artist Vision on but herself. And Winnie wasn't entirely happy with what she was observing.

Her restless tossing and turning.

The persistent churning of her stomach.

Winnie *should've* been happy to have another regular Wednesday in her treehouse. But she wasn't.

Late in the night, when Winnie's tossing and turning grew so agitated that Buttons kicked her out of bed with an annoyed *mew!* Winnie slumped down the loft steps to make herself some hot cocoa (the best kind, with the mini marshmallows). And that's when she noticed that the mailbox light on the wall was glowing red.

TRANSCRIPT

The following is what was said during a walkie-talkie conversation between Lyle and Winnie that took place late in the evening of Wednesday, May 3rd. 🌀

Winnie: Hello? Hello? Who's this walkie-talkie from? The note said "Press to Talk," so I did.

Lyle: Winnie! It's me, Lyle! You got our package! Do you like all the stuff we sent you? Over!

Winnie: Hi, Lyle! I'm going through the box now. Ooh, Cheetos treats! Nice.

Lyle, do you record <u>ALL</u> your walkie-talkie conversations?
—Squizzy

My stupid cousin was playing with a tape recorder outside my room and taped it by accident. Lucky for us, though, because now we can put it in this memoir!
—Lyle

Maybe your cousin's not so stupid after all.
—Squizzy

I wouldn't go <u>THAT</u> far.
—Lyle

Lyle: [after a pause] Were you done talking? When you're done talking, you're supposed to say "over." Over!

Winnie: Oh yeah, I was all done. Over!

Lyle: Cool. Yeah, so the Cheetos treats are from Aayush, obviously. We all wanted to put something in there for you—me and the other Treehouse Ten, I mean. To say thanks and stuff. Over!

Winnie: Wow, this is awesome. A friend-ship bracelet, a new travel Scrabble, some books. Ha, dental floss. Nice, Lyle. Oh, this stuffed lizard is great. Tabitha's getting really good at those. [pause] This is really nice, but what are you guys thanking me for? Over.

Lyle: Winnie, for someone so smart, sometimes you're really dumb. You think we wouldn't fig-ure out you were the reason Greta and Tabitha get to go to Craft Camp? The reason Joey is touring Nolan Blight's studio? Our parents told us, Winnie. We know you're the one who did all that for us. I can't believe you didn't say anything. It was really nice. So, thanks. Over.

Winnie: Oh. Well, you're welcome. I mean, you're not mad? Over.

Lyle: Why would we be mad that you did a bunch of nice stuff for us? Over.

Winnie: I don't know, just . . . You guys had all these demands, when you came up here. And you didn't end up getting any of them. Over.

Lyle: Oh. I didn't think about it that way. You know what? I am mad! Over.

Winnie: You are? Over.

Lyle: No, dummy! Sheesh. You didn't get us what we asked for, but you got us stuff we needed. That's even better. You're a good friend, Winnie. Over.

Winnie: You really think so? Over.

Lyle: Floss my teeth and hope to die. Although you'd be an even better friend if you'd go see the giant tooth exhibit with me. My moms are taking me after school tomorrow. Wanna come? Over.

Winnie: I think I'm gonna stay up here a little longer. Just until . . . Well, I don't know. Over.

Lyle: I get it. [pause] Hey, so, Winnie? I have to tell you something. You're not going to like it. Over.

Winnie: What is it? Oh, there's a whole pack of water balloons in here! Nice! And a brand-new *Super Joey*! Over.

Lyle: Yeah, so, Squizzy overheard her dad on the phone with this historian guy, and it turns out there's some old dumb law about embassies and consulates and . . . Okay, I didn't understand everything. But it turns out your treehouse really isn't its own country anymore. Your parents can make you come down anytime they want. Over.

[Long pause]

Lyle: Winnie? Winnie? Did you fall out the window? Do I need to call an ambulance? Over.

Winnie: [sigh] I'm here. Thanks for telling me. About the treehouse, I mean. I guess maybe I should . . . I don't know. Do my parents know already? How come they haven't come to get me down, do you think? Over.

Lyle: I don't know about your parents, Winnie. But I didn't tell you the other thing yet. The other thing is that I overheard my mom Dana on the phone today, too, talking to Logan and Brogan's dad. You know, the fancy lawyer? And get this. He said that, if you want, you can sue your own parents. Did you know that's a thing you can do? Over.

Winnie: Why would I sue my own parents? Over.

Lyle: Because then you can live all by yourself! Mr. Litz said you have a good case.

You'd be an "immaculate minor," or something like that. He said if you wanted he'd work on your case pro bozo. Over.

Winnie: Huh?

Lyle: You didn't say "over." Over!

Winnie: Oh, sorry. Huh? Over!

Lyle: That's better. Over.

Winnie: [sighs again] Lyle, what are you talking about? Over.

Lyle: I'm talking about how you can live in your treehouse forever! Even if it's not your own country! None of your parents' weird schedules or crazy holidays or anything anymore. You can do whatever you want, never worry about failing anything ever again. Isn't that great? Over.

[Another long pause]

Lyle: Winnie? Over?

Dad said it's called an "emancipated minor," which means a kid who gets to be in charge of himself, without his parents.
—Brogan

cool! you think dad would let us do that?
—logan

He said if we threw any more water balloons at him he'd "emancipate" us himself. (I think he was joking.)
—Brogan

✓ Dad said it's "pro bono," which means "for free."
—Brogan

✓ (brogan, you're a pro bozo!) ☺
—logan

Winnie: Yeah. Yeah, that's great, I guess. Over.

Lyle: You don't sound very happy. I thought you'd think it was good news. Over.

Winnie: No, it is. I mean, that's what I wanted from the beginning, right? Getting away from my parents being so weird all the time? Over.

Lyle: Hey, look, Winnie, I should probably go. It's pretty late, and no way I can be tardy tomorrow, because Mr. B is so mad that we all missed, like, two weeks of school. You know he gave us a pop quiz in lit today? Everyone failed, obviously. But he said he's coming up with some huge project for us all to do to make up for it. Something about a memoir? I asked him and he said there might possibly be enough for you to do to pass fifth grade, even without turning in your local history report, if you worked really hard. I don't know all the details yet, but . . . Well, it'd be cool to get to hang out with you in middle school. Don't you think? Over.

Winnie: Yeah. Sounds good, Lyle, thanks. Oh, and tell everyone else thanks for all the nice presents. The stuffed lizard and every- thing. Over.

Lyle: Of course. And, Winnie? Is there any- thing you need? Besides, like, water balloons and dental floss, I mean? 'Cause if there is, I'll totally help. Over.

Winnie: [pause] Actually . . . Maybe there is something. If you don't mind staying up just a little bit later. Over.

Lyle: What is it? I'll do anything. Over.

Winnie: How good are you at forging notes? Over.

Dear Mom,

It's me, Winnie! Can you come
to the treehouse to talk to
me? Come at exactly 9:00 a.m.
tomorrow (Thursday!), and
don't be late! I'm just inviting
you, not Dad!

Love,
Your daughter,
Winnie

P.S. If my handwriting looks
different, it's because I have
a cold.

Dear Dad,

Hey, Dad, it's Winnie, your daughter! I'm only writing to you, not Mom! I'm officially inviting you to come to the treehouse tomorrow morning exactly at 9:02 a.m. (Just you! Mom won't be there at all!) THE TIME IS REALLY IMPORTANT! 9:02.

(So you know, my writing might look weird because I sprained my hand eating Froot Loops.)

See you on Thursday! At 9:02!

Love,
Winnie

The Most Remarkable Thing

20 days after what happened happened

Winnie's parents weren't exactly thrilled that they'd been tricked into visiting the treehouse at the same time. But they stayed to talk anyway—because Winnie spun the lock on the trapdoor so quickly they couldn't escape.

"Winifred," her father said with a frown, "this subterfuge is beneath you. I have no intention of discussing *anything* with your *mother* present."

Winnie didn't know what *subterfuge* was, but she didn't care. "Well, then I hope you like Froot Loops," she said. "Because that's pretty much all there is left to eat. And I'm going to make you live here until you finally *do* decide to talk to me." She turned her gaze on her mom, who seemed about to protest just as loudly as Winnie's dad had. "You, too, Mom. And don't even *think* about using the zip line."

Winnie's mom *harrumph*ed. Her dad scowled. But they remained in their seats on the daybed, with Winnie standing before them, her arms crossed over her chest, like *she* was the parent and they were the bratty children.

"I've been very worried about you, you know, Winifred," her dad said. "I took several days off work, and stood at the kitchen window, just watching, to make sure you were okay in here. And you know, I hardly ever saw your mother watching out *her* window."

Winnie's mom slapped her hands on her knees. "You think you were more worried than I was?" she shouted at Winnie's dad. "I kept a worry *journal*. You want to see it? Winifred, let me out of here, I'm going to go on home and get my worry journal, so Varun can see which of us was more concerned about you."

"I don't care who was more concerned!" Winnie shouted. It seemed like a good time for shouting. "You think that matters? So you were worried about me? Great! You're *supposed* to be worried about me! You're my *parents*. That's your *job*!" Once the words started coming, Winnie found she couldn't have stopped them if she'd wanted to. "But you should've come *up* here. You should've tried to get me *down*. That's all I asked for, and you couldn't even do it."

"But—" her mom started.

"But—" her dad said.

Winnie cut them off. "You're here now," she said.

Both of her parents in the treehouse together—that was

the only thing Winnie had demanded when she'd climbed up into her treehouse and refused to come down. But once she'd turned her Artist Vision on herself and really examined things in the shifted light, she'd realized that what she *needed* was something more.

"I need you to listen to me," she told her parents. "Like, *really listen*."

It was not an easy conversation. Winnie's parents did not want to listen. What they wanted to talk about was holidays and schedules and who loved whom more and all sorts of ridiculous things. But Winnie didn't give up.

"*I want.*"

Winnie said that a lot.

"*I need.*"

Winnie said that, too.

"*I don't like.*"

Winnie's mom frowned. She brought up her plans for World Fish Migration Day at least twice, but Winnie scooped up Buttons and petted his soft fur and took his good advice and kept talking.

"*I want.*"

"*I need.*"

"*I don't like.*"

Winnie's dad growled. He mentioned the time when Winnie was five and her mother had lost track of her in the grocery store and Winnie had cried. (*"I've* never lost you in a grocery store," he said.) But Winnie tucked her chin into Buttons's orange neck and listened to his comforting purrs and kept talking.

"I want."

"I need."

"I don't like."

And eventually, a remarkable thing happened. It was, Winnie realized, the most remarkable thing that had happened since Winnie had first climbed up into her treehouse and refused to come down.

Winnie's parents began to listen.

They pinched their lips and they looked at their hands and they nodded their heads while Winnie spoke.

Buttons raised his kitty eyebrows at Winnie. She could tell he thought the development was pretty remarkable, too. Winnie scratched at his favorite spot and kept talking.

"I want."

"I need."

"I don't like."

When Winnie had said all the words she needed to say, she set Buttons down gently and she went to her parents, sitting there on the daybed, staring at their hands. And she hugged them. She didn't worry about who she was hugging first and who she was hugging second. She just hugged.

"I love you," she told her parents.

They sniffled up their tears.

They smoothed out their frowns.

Then they said the words that *they* needed to say.

"We love you, too."

That's what they said.

"We're sorry."

They said that, too.

And after all of those remarkable things, there was only one thing left to do.

"I think," Winnie told her parents, "I'm ready to leave the treehouse now."

JUNE!!

SUNDAY	MONDAY	TUESDAY
4 HUG YOUR CAT DAY! (Buttons says we have to celebrate!)	5	6 Drive-In Movie Day! 🌀
11 Going-Away Party with Mom!	12 Winnie and Dad in Kansas to study grouse poop!!!	13
18 Father's Day!	19	20
25 sleepover with Greta & Tabitha? ✗	26 Winnie and Mom's camping adventure! ✳	27 Canoe Day!

✗ Mom & Dad—OK?

✳ Don't forget to ask Jolee if you can borrow her sleeping bag!

🌀 W— Drive-In Movie Day sounds fun, I think! Want to celebrate the weekend before so you have more time to finish up your memoir? Ask L and S if they can join us? Love, Mom

WEDNESDAY	THURSDAY	FRIDAY	SATURDAY
	1	2 Jolee's Scrabble championship!!! (slumber party after)	3
7 *Winnie's Collective Memoir Due!!!!!!*	8	9 *WINNIE'S LAST DAY OF FIFTH GRADE!*	10 Lyle's pool party!!!
14	15	16	17
21 ✓	22 ONION RINGS DAY!	23	24 sleepover at Squizzy's!
28	29	30 Treehouse Ten treehouse reunion?	⚡ Mom & Dad—OK?

✓ Dad, want to try Go Skateboarding Day??

‖ *Winnie, any interest?*
Yes, please!

A Big Win

49 days after what happened happened

After Jolee won first place in the semiregional Scrabble tournament in May, she'd gone on to compete in the regional tournament. And then the statewide competition. And then, one week before the last day of fifth grade, Jolee and all the Treehouse Ten (and all their parents, too) found themselves at the Junior National Scrabble Championships.

Jolee blew everyone out of the water. Her first play in her final game was the word *equinox*, which earned her 116 points, and things only got better from there. Her grand-prize trophy was taller than she was, so when it came time to snap her photo, Jolee asked her little sister, Ainslee, to sit on top of her shoulders to help make things even. (Jolee said later that Ainslee could still be super annoying, but most of the time she didn't mind having her around as much.)

Winnie and her friends and all the parents cheered Jolee from the audience. Winnie's parents sat in separate rows and

20 points for a double-letter on the Q, plus 13 for the rest of the word, then double-word for starting on the star, and a 50-point bonus for using all my letters!
—Jolee

(Last time we played Scrabble, I got 8 points for "hop.")
—Lyle

✓

It's a pretty good photo, even if Ainslee IS giving me bunny ears!
—Jolee

didn't speak much, but Winnie was pretty proud of their behavior. Afterward, the Treehouse Ten were invited to join Jolee at her table at the winners' reception dinner, while the parents sat at a separate table. (Winnie could tell that her parents really didn't want to sit at the same table, but they did it anyway, without even grumbling, and Winnie was proud of them for that, too.)

It was while they were working on their salad course that the Treehouse Ten turned to the question of what they should call themselves. After all, Lyle pointed out, they didn't live in a treehouse anymore. "And we can't exactly go back to being the Tulip Street Ten, either, since we'll be in middle school." He speared a tomato on the end of his fork and added, "I mean, if Mr. B accepts our memoir and doesn't fail us. But I bet we're probably gonna pass fifth grade, don't you think?"

"How about Ten Kids Who Used to Hang Out All the Time?" Squizzy suggested, devouring a bread roll.

"Ten Kids Who *Still* Hang Out All the Time, Even Though They Go to Different Schools," Joey said. "Pass me the butter."

"How 'bout the Lizard People?" Tabitha piped up, and Greta offered her a high five for her great suggestion.

"Dragon Destroyers!" said Logan.

"*Dragon Destroyers* Destroyers!" said Brogan, which Logan thought was even better.

"Maybe," Winnie said thoughtfully, chewing on a bite of

Right, Mr. B?? We did a good job on this memoir, didn't we?????? —Lyle

lettuce. She paused to swallow, and the others waited to hear what she had to say. "Maybe we should just stick with the Treehouse Ten? I mean, I know we don't live there anymore, but I bet that's what the world will always remember us by."

Lyle raised his water glass. "I like it!" he said, and they all clinked their glasses together.

"Hey, Winnie?" Squizzy said. "What would you say to a slumber party in the treehouse sometime? With all of us, I mean? We've been talking and we sort of miss it. Now that it's in the United States again, I bet our parents would actually let us go. And I promise not to make any timetables or anything."

The very thought of another slumber party with her friends—a real one, not a two-week-long one—made Winnie happy all over. "That would be fun," she said. She took another bite of salad. "Plus"—she paused to chew—"you guys could help me work on a project I've been thinking about. Something to do with the treehouse, so it doesn't just sit there so empty all the time. But . . ." Winnie added up that month's calendar days in her head. "It would mean taking away one of my mom's days with me this month, and she's gonna get way less than my dad anyway, because of us going to Kansas. And I know my dad's sort of bummed about me coming back early, to spend the *rest* of the summer with my mom, so . . ." Winnie spun her blue-and-gold friendship bracelet around her wrist—the one Greta had made her special at Craft Camp. At last she nodded. "All

I can do is ask, right?" she said to her friends. And when the Treehouse Ten agreed, Winnie stood up, took a deep breath, and went to talk to her parents.

Her parents, when she talked to them, took pretty deep breaths, too.

But they listened, which was all Winnie could ask them to do.

"I think that sounds reasonable." That's what Winnie's mom said, after thinking about it for a few seconds. She didn't even frown, either. "It's fine with me, if your father agrees."

"I bet you'd have a lot of fun, wouldn't you?" Winnie's dad replied. "Why don't you go ahead and put it on the calendar?"

Winnie hadn't used her Artist Vision in a while, but she turned it on then, just for practice. She squinted her eyes, observing her parents in the shifted light.

The twitch of her mom's lip, just before her mouth morphed into a smile.

The smirk in her dad's eyes, as he watched his daughter.

Winnie's dad pulled a notebook out of his back pocket then and flipped a few pages. "Do you have a moment, Winifred?" he asked. "I wanted to go over the plans I've been drafting for Hug Your Cat Day. How do you think Buttons would feel about wearing a full-body cat suit?"

Winnie's mom slapped a palm to her forehead. "Oh, *Varun*," she groaned. But then she let out a laugh, thick and cheerful.

Yep, Winnie thought, after giving her mom and dad each a quick peck on the cheek and scuttling off to rejoin her friends. Her parents were still her parents—always would be.

But for the first time in what felt like ages, Winnie found that she didn't mind too much.

How to Be a Scrabble Champ

by Jolee Watson

#1: Memorization

If you want to win big at Scrabble, you need to start memorizing uncommon words that will score you lots of points! Some good words are JUKEBOX, for a minimum 77 points, or SQUIFFY ("slightly tipsy"), for a minimum 75. And don't forget about two-letter words! You can do a lot of damage with a word like XI (the fourteenth letter of the Greek alphabet).

#2: Addition

It's not always about having great letters—sometimes the best way to score is to add onto a word that's already there. Turning CHILD into CHILDISH or WRITE into COWRITE can boost your score with just a few letters.

#3: Blocking

To be really good at Scrabble, you can't just look out for yourself. You need to keep an eye on your opponent, too.

So even if it sounds mean, you have to make sure that he (or she) can't score off any really big squares. If you can't use that triple-word square for yourself, block it with a word that can't be added onto!

#4: Support

It definitely doesn't hurt to have awesome friends who will find semiregional tournaments for you to compete in (thanks, Winnie!) and who come to the Junior National Finals to cheer you on, screaming as loud as they can when all you have is six vowels and a B. (Treehouse Ten Forever!!!)

TRANSCRIPT

The following is what was said on the Channel 10 Action News special report that aired on the evening of Tuesday, June 6th, just before the end of the school year:

Amanda Howard, Channel 10 Action News Correspondent: This is Amanda Howard, live with local celebrity Gwenyth Mahadi-Magage, otherwise known as the Girl from the Treehouse. Hi, Gwinnie, thanks for joining us today.

Winnie: Um, my name's Winnie, actually.

Frank Quijata, Channel 10 Action News Cameraman: [voice heard off camera] *I told you, Amanda.*

Amanda Howard: Oh, Frankie, hush. You don't know everything. [smiles at Winnie] We're here to do a follow-up piece with you, now that your treehouse has been officially declared part of the United States. Were you so sad to leave?

Winnie: I guess a little. It was nice to live there for a while, but getting back to normal is good, too.

Amanda Howard: And do you ever go back to the treehouse these days?

Winnie: Sure. Even if I don't live there, it's a great place to hang out. I spend afternoons with my friends there sometimes or with my uncle Huck or sometimes even one of my parents will come, and we do art projects or whatever. Some days I go up with just my cat, Buttons. He's the greatest cat in the whole—

Amanda Howard: Sounds delightful. I love dogs, too. But in more important news, I hear you and your classmates are writing a memoir about your time in the treehouse?

Winnie: Yeah, we're submitting it for the "Your Class Writes!" competition. We've been working *really* hard. It's due tomorrow, so we're almost done. Our teacher told us we had to do a really good job on it or he wouldn't let us graduate, since we missed so much school.

But I think he'll pass us. I don't want to brag, but I think it turned out pretty nice. 🌀

Amanda Howard: Well, I do hope you all don't fail miserably. But back to the treehouse. What's this I hear about a museum?

Winnie: [surprised] Oh. Well, it's just an idea I had. Nothing's final yet. But I was thinking, since we all had so much fun in the treehouse, it might be cool to let other kids hang out there, too, sometimes. My friends and I are still working on the details, and my uncle Huck's going to help with the design, but our basic idea is to turn the treehouse into a fun zone, where any kid can come visit. Like, there will be a reading space in the loft, and you can read any books you find there or bring books for other kids to find. That was Squizzy's idea. Or you can work on food experiments in the kitchen. Aayush has all sorts of plans for that. There's going to be a comic-book-making area and a craft space and a board-game zone, and some days there will be water balloon fights. You'll know when those are scheduled so you'll only get

It did, right, Mr. B???
We can pass 5th
grade, right????

— Squizzy

drenched if you want. And, for those kids out there who are super into teeth, my friend Lyle is going to host a series on dental hygiene. He's working on a PowerPoint and everything.

Amanda Howard: It sounds lovely, except for that last part, about the teeth.

Frank Quijata: [voice heard off camera] *Be nice, Amanda. I think it all sounds wonderful, Winnie!*

Amanda Howard: Please ignore Frankie, Gwindovere. He never knows what he's talking about. *Anyway*, before we turn back to the studio, can you tell us when this treehouse fun zone will be open to the public?

Winnie: Sure. We're hoping to open it by the beginning of next school year. We're all going to be pretty busy, obviously, with middle school and everything—well, I hope!—so it won't be an everyday thing. But once it's open, any kid can drop by and visit, and it'll only cost two dollars to enter. [smiles at camera] The treehouse will be open every Wednesday.

Dear Winnie, Lyle, Squizzy, Tabitha, Aayush, Jolee, Logan, Greta, Joey, and Brogan,

Well, I really wish you hadn't missed all that school back in April, but I have to admit this memoir is very well done. Excellent work, everyone! I enjoyed getting to know all of you better, and I hope the folks at the publishing contest will, too. (I'm no judge, but I think they'd be crazy to pick anyone else's entry over yours!)

I will very much miss you all when you head off to middle school next year. Please do stay in touch and let me know what fabulous things you get up to. It's been a real pleasure teaching you all this year (and learning a lot from you, too!).

Yours truly,
Mr. Hector Benetto

P.S. In case it wasn't clear, you all passed. A-pluses for everyone! That includes you, Winnie—I can tell you worked very hard on this!

P.P.S. Please remember to remove all of the Post-it notes throughout before you submit this to the contest!